MW01658063

"I'm finally going to be married!"

Caroline could only stand there looking at them, not believing what she was seeing. A horrible twisting pain splintered her heart, and the room swayed and tilted.

She saw David untangle himself from Sharon's embrace, taking a step toward her. "Caroline!" she heard as if from a great distance.

He would never know what it cost her to stand and face them with such resolute calmness when everything inside her was dissolving. *He knew how much she loved him. How could he do this to her?*

"Congratulations. I wish you every happiness." She almost managed to smile at him.

She told herself he belonged to Sharon. She had to start now to make sure there'd be no awkward ghosts between them for him to remember once he became her brother-in-law.

Books by Maura McGiveny

HARLEQUIN PRESENTS

674—A GRAND ILLUSION
723—PROMISES TO KEEP
803—ALMOST A BRIDE

HARLEQUIN ROMANCE

2511—DUQUESA BY DEFAULT
2679—MEGAN'S FOLLY

These books may be available at your local bookseller.

Don't miss any of our special offers. Write to us at the following address for information on our newest releases.

MAURA MCGIVENY

almost a bride

Harlequin Books

TORONTO • NEW YORK • LONDON
AMSTERDAM • PARIS • SYDNEY • HAMBURG
STOCKHOLM • ATHENS • TOKYO • MILAN

Harlequin Presents first edition July 1985
ISBN 0-373-10803-6

Original hardcover edition published in 1985
by Mills & Boon Limited

Printed in U.S.A.

CHAPTER ONE

CAROLINE tucked the blanket around her brother and gently kissed him good night. He yawned sleepily, curling his arm around a bedraggled teddy bear.

''Night, Caro,' he murmured.

''Night, darling. Sleep tight.' Smoothing back his dark hair, she turned towards the door, leaving it open a crack in case he should wake again and call out for her.

She slipped her hands in the pockets of her flannel dressing gown and tiptoed down the dim hallway. She wasn't worried about disturbing her father or her two other brothers sleeping in the big upstairs bedrooms of their rambling farmhouse. They were the least of her problems. One irascible old grandfather caused her more trouble than all the others. If she could only get past his door without waking him . . .

'Caroline? Is that you wandering round at this hour?' her grandfather called.

She froze for a moment then sighed before pushing open his door and sticking her head inside. 'Sorry. I had to settle Tim,' she said lightly. 'He had a nightmare again. I'm just going downstairs to make sure all the doors are locked then I'll turn in.'

He sat up in bed and flicked on the bedside lamp, his dark eyes peering at the clock on his nightstand before looking back at her. Bushy white eyebrows rose in mock surprise. 'And what's Sharon supposed to do when she finally gets home? Crawl in the pantry window?'

With a small sound of exasperation, her shoulders slumped and she came to the side of his bed. 'How did you know she'd gone out?'

'You have to get up pretty early in the morning to fool me. Besides, I heard her on the 'phone to the Pengelly girl this afternoon.'

She sat down on the edge of his bed and smiled gently, taking one of his gnarled hands in both of hers. 'It's not really that late. Don't worry about her.'

'How can a man not worry about his grandchildren? I may be old but I'm not dead.'

'Sharon said she wouldn't be late,' she soothed. 'I'm not worried. You shouldn't be either.'

'Where that girl's concerned, I'm always worried. Look at the time. Midnight already. She may be the oldest of all of you but when it comes to brains, she missed out on her share.'

'Now, Grandy, you know Daddy always said twenty-five's too old for a curfew.'

'I don't care what your father said. For all the notice he takes of things around here now, he might as well have died along with your mother.' His eyes clouded and he looked at his tall slender granddaughter with her dark brown hair braided and draped over her shoulder. 'Sharon's irresponsible, that's what she is. She knows you have to get up at the crack of dawn to get things going and see that the boys get off to school all right but does she care that she's interfering with your rest? It isn't right and I'm not going to put up with it.'

'Grandy, please,' she cut in, squeezing his hand gently, knowing once he got started he'd work himself into a fine rage and never get back to sleep. Her voice was deliberately low and soothing. 'I don't mind missing a little sleep. And Sharon asked before she left. I told her to go.'

'That doesn't make it right.' His face twisted morosely. 'Things have got to change around here. This family's hanging together by a thread. What if something happens to me? Who'll take care of things then? If you'd got yourself married like you were supposed to last year, we'd have a man around here and I could rest easy.'

A cold hand squeezed her heart, aggravating the wound that had never completely healed. She got to her feet and kept her face expressionless with an effort. 'But Philip didn't marry me so we just have to make the best of it,' she said flatly, not wanting to hear any more.

He refused to let it go. 'How can we make the best of something like that?'

'Grandy——'

'Look at you, Caroline. I know you're putting on a good front but I remember the girl you used to be: sweet, outgoing, smiling all the time. Now you're little more than a shadow round here. How long since you laughed? You've cut yourself off from everything outside this family. You never go out. You have no friends.'

'I do have friends——'

'I'm not talking about that idiot, Morwenna Polzion. I'm talking about men friends.'

'I've got you and Daddy and the boys. You're all the men I need.'

'That's what I mean. You won't even look at any man outside this family. You need someone and I need him too. If only your mother were still alive. She'd know how to reach you.' His eyes took on a sad, faraway look. 'If only Philip hadn't left you standing at the altar.'

Her breath left her in an exasperated rush and her chin shot up instinctively. He was always trying to get her to talk about it. He couldn't understand how she could go on like nothing happened after that blow to her pride. Anyone else would have gone away where no one knew her to start over. But she was made of sterner stuff. For more than a year now, gossip made her a pariah, a social outcast, but she was determined to ignore it. At first Grandy was protective but then, as time went on and he saw she wouldn't tolerate his sympathy, he tried other, sometimes cruel, tactics to bring it out in the open. She wouldn't talk to him about it even though she knew he was waiting for her to come to him. She had been hurt but she chose to keep it to herself.

Her voice was even. 'There are some things we can't change. We simply have to learn to accept them. Mum died and I didn't get married and Daddy's retreated into his own little world. Let's just leave it at that, shall we? I'll go check and see if Sharon's home yet and bring you some warm milk to help you sleep.'

'Warm milk.' His lip curled before he slid back down beneath his blanket. 'I can do without that, thank you.'

'Oh, Grandy.' She sighed again and impulsively bent her head and kissed him on the cheek, trying not to flinch when he roughly pulled away from her. Her voice was husky. 'I know you're concerned and I love you for it but I can handle things. I'm a big girl now.'

'Twenty-one and you think you know everything,' he muttered.

Trying to contain her exasperation, she switched off his light and left him. There was no getting through to him in this mood so the best thing to do was ignore it and hope he'd be more amenable in the morning.

Everything was quiet and still when she went down to the cosy kitchen with its big scrubbed table and old-fashioned woodburning stove. The fire was out and she wrapped her arms around herself to ward off the chill. But the coldness was from inside and she knew it. If only Grandy knew, he didn't have to keep reminding her about being left at the altar. It was never very far from her thoughts and this was the time of the day it always came rushing back, full force, to haunt her.

She could still see Philip Tregenna when she closed her eyes. He had been so handsome, tall and dark with black hair and almost equally black eyes. He was kind and generous. His smile could charm the birds out of the trees and her father loved him like a son. Everybody loved him. No one could know him and not love him. But with Caroline, it had been to quick and too consuming to be real. She met him and was swept off her feet, dazzled by the sheer force and power of his personality. She didn't know what love was all about then.

'Beware the dark stranger,' her best friend,

Morwenna Polzion, said, frowning strangely at the tea leaves in the bottom of Caroline's cup only the day before her wedding. 'He's going to break your heart.'

Little did she know twenty-four hours later she'd be standing at the back of the little village church, waiting for the tall dark groom who never showed up.

'But he wasn't a stranger!' she told Morwenna, her only bridesmaid, the only one who shared all her secrets.

Morwenna just rolled her eyes and said quite softly: 'Yes he was. You thought you loved him but you didn't really know anything about him. You loved the dream not the man.'

She wanted to die at the time but nothing could be that easy. The guests awkwardly left the church with confused and sympathetic murmurings and with the long white skirts of her wedding gown trailing limply in the dust, Caroline made her way alone to the cemetery and threw herself on the gently blowing grass covering her mother's grave.

'Why, Mum, why?' Bitter scalding tears blinded her and her heart shattered. There was no comforting presence she had always felt before. There were no answers this time.

She never knew how long she stayed there but the sun was slanting long shadows on the gravestones when her father finally found her and lifted her to her feet and stumblingly took her home. He didn't say anything. His face was deathly pale and fixed.

A long time after that, Morwenna told her that her father had gone to Philip's home that day and talked to him. He never told anyone what they said to each other. He never told Caroline why Philip failed to show up at the church or why he left the country two days later. News filtered back from America that he died there six weeks later. The only thing her father said to her was: 'He wasn't the man for you, my love. He would have ended up breaking your heart.'

So Caroline was left, if not with a broken heart, with one that was bruised beyond repair. Philip Tregenna hurt not only her but also her father. Whatever Philip told him that day, he had never been the same after hearing it. Little by little he withdrew. Now he sat and stared vacantly into space and Caroline cared for him as if he was one of her brothers.

Standing now at the kitchen window, so tall and still and straight, she listened to the rising wind sending the waves to break against the huge granite boulders at the bottom of the cliffs in the distance and was comforted by the sound. She loved this majestic open stretch of Cornish coastline where she lived. Her life here might not be the easiest, trying to care for three young boys and two men with her older sister on this tiny farm outside Penzance, but she refused to take the easy way out and leave them. The humiliation wasn't hers alone. She stayed and faced it with her family. She knew her brothers were still fending off the pitying looks and unkind remarks from gossipy neighbours who wouldn't let it die. She didn't complain. This was her cross to bear. She wouldn't let herself dwell on how heavy it was.

A small sound at the doorway had her turning and she looked at her sister coming in before her eyes widened disbelievingly in the stunned silence.

Sharon smoothed her hands nervously over the limp black curls hanging on her shoulders and huge tears welled up in her eyes. 'Oh, Caroline! Look at me! What am I going to do?' She threw herself into her arms. 'I look so awful with black hair!'

It took Caroline a full minute to gather her scattered wits before she patted her on the back and held her away, trying not to wince at the offending greenish black dye job. Sharon was always so beautiful. More often than not Caroline felt gawky and graceless in comparison. 'Whatever possessed you to dye it?'

'I wanted to look like Judith,' Sharon wailed.

'Judith!' She was flabbergasted. 'Judith *who*?'

'Tremain,' she hiccupped. 'Remember how beautiful she was? And how much David loved her?'

Bewildered, Caroline stared at her with wide eyes and spread her hands helplessly. 'But Judith Tremain is dead! She had been for . . . what, two years now?'

'Three,' Sharon said, scrubbing at her eyes.

'Then what on earth's made you suddenly want to look like her?'

'David's back. Kathy Pengelly saw him yesterday in the cemetery visiting Judith's grave. He told her his travels were over. He's home to stay now.'

Caroline closed her eyes and let out a long slow breath. David Tremain. The answer to every woman's dream. At least he was six years ago before he went to America. He was handsome enough, she supposed, remembering him through a fifteen year old's eyes. He was twenty-five then and all the older girls were crazy about him—especially Sharon. He had dated her a few times but that was before he married Judith and took her to America.

Judith had everything: looks, personality, wealth, that indefinable elusive something that brought out a man's protective instincts. She should have had all the other girls green with envy but they weren't. Everyone loved her. So small and fragile, even now the remembrance of her tinkling laugh made

Caroline think of a hushed wind sighing through a hundred bell towers.

She blinked open her eyes again and looked at Sharon and shook her head. 'You thought if you made yourself look like Judith, David would notice you and come calling again?'

She nodded miserably. 'Well, wouldn't he?'

Caroline bit back an unkind retort. Aside from the fact that Sharon was a foot taller than Judith and a good twenty-five pounds heavier, it would take more than long black hair to remind David of his dead wife when he looked at her. 'No, I don't think so,' she said gently. 'You're altogether different. You don't look anything like her. Besides, don't you realise you'd only be putting more obstacles in your way? When he looked at you, you'd never know if he was seeing you or pretending you were Judith. You have to be yourself, Sharon. That's the only way.'

'Oh, Caro.' Her face crumpled and she dragged her hands through her hair. 'I knew I should have asked what you thought first. You're always so level headed. But it seemed so simple at Kathy's house. Her mother's hair dye was there on the shelf and we got to talking and somehow it was the perfect thing to do. Now it looks so awful. Grandy'll kill me!'

Caroline made a sympathetic sound and

wondered how she was going to salvage this one. 'No he won't,' she soothed. 'He may roar a bit but he won't kill you.'

'You know how he's always telling me I don't have both oars in the water? Well, I think he's right. I shouldn't have been so stupid. What am I going to do?'

She smothered a small laugh, glad she wasn't going to be the recipient of Grandy's cutting wit this time. 'Let's put the kettle on, shall we? Between us, we ought to think of something . . .'

When Grandy finished the milking and came in for breakfast the next morning, he pulled out his chair with a preoccupied frown not looking at anyone. Everyone else was already seated at the long kitchen table and it was only after he noticed the unnatural silence all around him that he looked up, his eyes going from eight-year-old Tim on his left, to fourteen-year-old Rob next to him, to sixteen-year-old Michael. Their eyes were glued to their plates as he glared balefully at their innocent faces. Then he focused his attention on Caroline sitting at the foot of the table calmly sipping her coffee. His eyebrows descended in a thunderous frown when he searched her carefully blank expression. Next to her was her father, Grandy's son, Alexander Pentreath. A tall slender man, he sat staring straight ahead with vacant eyes, seeing, hearing nothing. Sharon sat on the other side of her father and when Grandy finally got to her, his jaw sagged open and his eyes widened so much they nearly popped out of his head.

Her shoulder length hair had been cut in a short bob and it really didn't look too bad curling about her face in fine feathery wisps. Caroline was no hairdresser but, given the lateness of the hour and the anxiety she was feeling, she had done her best. At any rate, Sharon seemed pleased with the result and the horrible black dye didn't look quite so green this morning.

'*Sharon Pentreath.*' Grandy's voice was too controlled, too quiet. His fork clattered on to his plate and his napkin was practically hurled on to the table beside it. 'Come with me!'

'But Grandy, she's going to drive the boys to school——' Caroline began, only to be silenced by one impaling look from him.

Sharon gulped and got to her feet, throwing her sister a drowning look when she followed him out of the kitchen.

'What's he going to do to her?' Tim said fearfully, his eyes as big as saucers.

'He's going to tell her how stupid she is.' Michael leaned back in his chair and expelled his breath, putting his hands flat on the table. 'Her hair was pretty until she messed it up with that black dye.' He looked at Caroline who was stirring sugar into her father's coffee. 'You never did tell us why she did it. Wasn't plain old ordinary Pentreath brown good enough for her?'

'Of course it was,' she said quietly, throwing a reassuring smile at Tim. Of all her brothers, he was the only one who didn't understand Grandy. Yet. 'She just wanted a change, that's all. She feels as bad as we do that it didn't turn out beautiful but maybe with it cut short, it'll grow out fast. Now finish your breakfast,' she said briskly, 'or you'll be late for school'

Tim looked startled. 'You mean Sharon's still going to drive us?'

'Of course she is. Grandy's just giving her a piece of his mind, that's all. She'll be back in a minute.'

Rob's eyes danced with mischief and an irrepressible grin spread across his face as he started to get up from his chair.

She knew what was coming. 'Don't say it, Rob,' she admonished.

But he couldn't resist the temptation. 'If he keeps on giving people a piece of his mind, he's not going to have any left for himself,' he gurgled.

Michael laughed out loud and Tim giggled. A smile tugged at the sides of Caroline's mouth but she kept it firmly under control. She was supposed to be the adult in charge here and it wouldn't do for them to see her enjoying the joke at her grandfather's expense. 'That's enough, Rob.'

'Sorry,' he laughed, not one bit contrite.

'Go on, all of you. It's getting late.' Her voice was brisk when she rose to her feet and began clearing the table. 'Mike, will you take Daddy out to the garden before you go?' She looked at her father staring vacantly into space and pain came and went in her eyes. When she shaved him this morning, she had missed a place on his upper lip. 'It's sunny and the fresh air will do him good. Oh, and make sure his sweater's buttoned, will you? The calendar says almost May but it's still chilly.'

When they had gone and the dishes were done, Grandy came back and roughly pulled out a chair at the table. Caroline carefully put a cup of coffee in front of him and started to tiptoe away when he stopped her.

'What's Morwenna Polzion's 'phone number?' he said through his teeth.

Her eyes opened wide and she spun around. That was the last thing she expected him to say. 'Morwenna's?'

'You heard me,' he glared at her. 'I've got to get someone over here to care for you children—and someone to help me run this farm as well.'

'But I thought you didn't like her!' She sank into a chair beside him at a loss.

'Try using your head for once,' he

breathed harshly. 'I don't expect her to keep house for us. It's just that she's the biggest gossip I know. If I tell her I'm looking for someone, it'll spread all over the world like wildfire.'

He was exaggerating, she knew, but he never would admit he had a soft spot for her best friend. Morwenna did talk a lot but being a forty-five year old widow who lived alone in a small cottage at the edge of the cliffs, she must have her lonely moments. No one could blame her for being friendly.

'You're not being very kind, Grandy.'

'I'm not in the mood to be kind.' He ran a hand over his face and through his hair, making it stand up in stiff white spikes. 'Why did that nitwit have to dye her hair? And why did you cut it? That only made it worse. You both ought to have your heads examined.'

She squirmed in her chair. 'Sharon didn't explain?'

All of a sudden he became very still and his eyes narrowed, searching her guarded expression. 'No. All she did was cry. She must have told you, though. She did, didn't she? All right, out with it. Why?'

She lifted her shoulders helplessly. How could she betray Sharon's confidence like that? It would only make her sister look that much more stupid. 'Who knows why she does anything?' she said with false brightness. 'She said the dye was handy and it seemed a good thing to do at the time but when she got home, she realised it was a mistake. We cut it because we thought it wouldn't look quite so green and maybe it would grow out faster that way.'

He shook his head and let out a savage breath knowing she was covering up the real reason and he'd never get it out of her. 'It can't grow out fast enough for me. She looks like a plucked chicken now. And that only proves my point. You're not old enough to look after yourself, let alone the rest of us. You need someone here to keep you in line.'

'Grandy, I'm doing the best I can.' Her voice was very small.

'Your best isn't good enough.' At her barely hidden look of hurt, he breathed in deeply. 'I know you're trying hard to take your mother's place but it's no good. My mind's made up. I'm getting a housekeeper for you and a hired hand for myself. That will leave you and Sharon free . . .' his lips twisted, '. . . to look for husbands.'

'Oh please! Don't say that!'

His mouth shook with sudden compunction but he kept his voice gruff with an effort. 'Your life isn't over, Caroline, so don't pretend it is. You've been hurt but you're young and you'll bounce back. And never mind that nonsense you're always quoting about "If you never say hello, you won't have to say goodbye",' he jeered.

'There's a man out there just waiting for you. You'll never find him if I don't make you start looking.'

She buried her face in her hands and shook her head. Didn't he understand anything?

CHAPTER TWO

THERE was no arguing with him so she didn't try. Sharon might be thrilled at the prospect of looking for a husband but Caroline was quietly determined to forego that pleasure. Within a week, the first of the applicants for housekeeper started arriving for interviews. Where they came from, she couldn't imagine. But it was obvious after the first few that it wasn't going to work out. Some of them were too young—younger even than Caroline—and with no experience. And some were too old.

'I'm not running an old folks' home or a kindergarten,' Grandy grumbled, watching one woman depart, cane in hand, Michael having to help her into a rusting, dilapidated car. Grandy sat at the kitchen table, muttering darkly, his hands running distractedly across his chin. 'Aren't there any sane, ordinary, middle-aged women left in the world?'

Caroline busied herself at the stove, a small grin spreading across her face. She knew Morwenna was doing it deliberately. She just wondered how long it would take Grandy to realise it.

A firm knock at the back door startled her and Grandy looked up with a scowl.

'Another lunatic, no doubt. Show her in, Caroline.'

But it wasn't another unsuitable woman. She opened the screen door and looked up into David Tremain's handsome craggy face. As tall as Caroline was, David was easily a head and shoulders taller. His hair was darker than she remembered. Stylishly long and slightly waving, it was the colour of water-darkened sand and his eyes were brightly blue with laugh lines crinkling at the corners.

'Hello—Caroline?' he said softly, his low voice spilling into the kitchen like a gently lapping wave.

'You remembered me!' Unaccustomed pleasure shot through her and a sudden breathless awareness rippled down her spine drawing her to him like a magnet.

'How could I ever forget Sharon's little sister?' The laugh lines deepened when he smiled. 'You're quite grown up now and more beautiful than ever.'

Her senses tingled and a delicate blush ran up her neck before she took herself to task. If she wasn't careful, it would be so fatally easy to fall under his spell like all the other girls had done before her. He was a man and he had the power to hurt her. She hadn't thought it possible that anyone could breach her defences after all this time and after everything that had happened to her with Philip. But David had done it without even trying and with only a smile. 'Now I remember why Sharon was always so crazy about you,' she said lightly, erasing the unconscious stiffening of her expression and stepping firmly back behind her air of cool reserve. 'America hasn't changed you. You're still the same charming devil you always were.'

He laughed good naturedly and stepped farther into the kitchen. 'But you've changed, haven't you? You're taller and lovelier and suddenly able to speak up for yourself.'

She had to smile at that. 'It comes from living with Grandy.' Looking at her grandfather still seated at the table, she said softly, 'You remember David Tremain, Grandy?'

'Mr Pentreath.' David walked to the table and shifted his wide brimmed hat to his left hand, extending his right to him. He was dressed in well-worn jeans and a blue plaid shirt and Grandy raised his eyebrows when his big hand was warmly clasped.

'Well, well. David Tremain. Come to call on Sharon, have you?'

'Not this time,' he said gently. 'I heard you were looking for help.'

Grandy's eyebrows rose even higher and his eyes widened. '*You* want to help me?'

He nodded. 'Is there some reason why I shouldn't?'

'Uh, no,' he blustered. 'It's just—I thought—sit down, sit down, my boy. Caro, get David a cup of coffee.'

Caroline was amazed. She had never seen Grandy discomfited before. He was actually fidgeting in his chair.

'I haven't been to see my father-in-law yet,' David said quietly as if that explained everything. He pulled out a chair and easily settled his big frame into it. 'My son and I are staying with Morwenna.'

Grandy let out a small sigh and nodded and Caroline became more and more intrigued. If David had been back in the country for more than a week already, why hadn't he seen his father-in-law? He had no family of his own left in Cornwall, that much she knew. There were only some distant cousins in Wales. If she had been in his shoes, Judith's home would have been the first place she'd go. Judith's father, Sir James Treloar, rattled around that big mansion of his. He must be lonely and dying to see his grandson after all this time. As far as she knew, he had never seen him. Steven had been born in America just a few months after Judith left.

She stopped dead and her eyes widened as all at once it hit her. She'd only been fifteen at the time so the gossip hadn't meant much to her then but now she realised why Judith's precipitate marriage to David had caused such a sensation up and down the coast. Judith must have already been pregnant, and in fleeing to America she hoped to avoid the scandal.

Her lips twisted and sympathy flared. Judith should have known better. Sir James had virtually become a recluse since then. Most likely it was because of the gossip.

Swallowing jerkily, she set a cup of coffee in front of David, pulling the sugar and cream jug towards him. Her eyes met his for a fraction of a second and that was all it took for him to read the sudden knowledge in them.

A look of regret rippled across his face when he gravely thanked her then he turned his attention back to Grandy.

'It's not that the work is so hard or that there's so much to do around here,' Grandy was saying. 'The boys do help after school but I'm not as young as I used to be. And then there's my son,' hc sighed painfully.

David nodded with compassion. 'Morwenna told me about him. I'm sorry.' He flicked an unreadable look at Caroline.

She knew he must have heard a twisted version of her being left at the altar and how it changed her father. Her chin lifted coldly, in faint challenge, daring him to say anything.

But David didn't respond.

'Yes, well,' Grandy pulled himself together. 'The job's yours if you want it. Will you be needing room and board as well as the salary I'm offering? There's plenty of room in this rambling old house.'

David gave him a slow understanding smile. 'I think Morwenna lives close enough not to make it a problem getting here. She says she likes looking after us. It brings out her motherly instincts.'

Grandy's lips twisted almost to a sneer. 'I'll give you a word of advice about that woman. Don't go letting her run your life for you or fill your head with any of her psychic nonsense. Drink coffee instead of tea—that way she can't read the leaves and tell what dire things await you.'

David chuckled softly. 'She does tend to do that, doesn't she?' Draining his cup, he stood up to leave, flashing an easy grin at Caroline. 'Tell Sharon I'm sorry I missed her.' He shook Grandy's hand. 'I'll be back this evening to help with the milking.'

'Fine, my boy, fine.' He looked at Caroline then back to David. 'It'll be good to have someone to rely on again.'

A week passed before Caroline found the time to visit Morwenna to thank her for sending David to them. The farm work was running smoothly and Grandy was smiling again and had given up his search for a housekeeper for the moment. He never said as much. The applicants simply stopped coming. It wasn't mentioned any more and Caroline breathed easier.

Situated near Cornwall's more scenic, tumbling cliffs, Morwenna's cottage was always warm and welcoming. Half-timbered, it was small and white, surrounded by a riot of colourful violets mixed with sea-pinks and bluebells and hung with wisteria. Her lawn was kept like a soft green velvet carpet and her pride and joy, a thatched roof, was something of a local tourist attraction.

Caroline took the long way there this morning, following the rocky cliff path, letting the murmuring slap-slap of the sea match her mood. It was a glorious morning and she was glad to be alive.

Morwenna was sitting in her sunny garden with a dark haired little boy kneeling in the blowing grass in front of her having his palm read. 'A lovely lady will come into your life and you'll love her like a mother . . .' she was murmuring in her low musical voice. 'Her eyes will hold all the mysteries of the sea. And her smile . . . watch for her smile. That's how you'll know her.'

'Hello, Morwenna,' Caroline called from the gate before lifting the latch and coming up the flower-lined walk. 'I thought I might find you out here. It's such a gorgeous day.'

'Come in, come in, Caro.'

The little boy quickly jumped to his feet and turned around to look at her.

'Steven Tremain, this is Caroline Pentreath,' she said when Caroline reached them.

'How do you do?' Steven stood rigidly erect, his expression solemn.

Caroline blinked, slightly taken aback by his formality. David was quiet but not unusually so, and her brothers and their friends were outgoing and boisterous. She had forgotten how shy some children could be. Thinking it might be her height intimidating him, she got down on her knees and looked him straight in the eye, flashing him a dazzling smile to put him at ease. 'Hello, Steven. How nice to meet you at last. Sharon's told me so much about you, I feel I know you already.'

Almost automatically he put his hand in both of hers, never taking his eyes off her smile. Then all at once his head swivelled to Morwenna and his bright blue eyes became big and round and full of questioning wonder.

A small knowing smile came and went across Morwenna's face and she nodded sagely but didn't say anything.

'A lovely lady,' he repeated almost reverently. 'And her eyes *are* like the sea. They're even the same colour, kind of bluey but green! How did you know?' He looked at his grubby little palm as if it could tell him something then he looked back at Caroline and grinned from ear to ear. 'Do you like snakes?' he ventured.

All of a sudden she let out an unconsciously held breath and laughed, giving an expressive shudder. 'Only if I see them coming and prepare myself. Yesterday I found one Tim left in his pocket before I washed his jeans. It scared me half to death.'

Steven chuckled and helped her to her feet, brushing the grass from her jeans. 'The same thing happened to my Dad once. He jumped a foot but then he said he wasn't really scared. He just didn't know it was there.' His solemn expression was completely erased by an irrepressible grin. 'I found a neat one yesterday and Morwenna gave me a box to keep him in. Would you like to see him?'

'All right,' she said bravely, hoping it was the common garden variety favoured by her brothers and not something that would scare the wits out of her.

'Go with him, Caro. I'll make some tea and then we'll talk.' Morwenna stood up and turned towards the house, her tidy little figure neat and trim in a blue flowered sun dress. A broad streak of silver threaded the dark strands of hair at her temples. Age had begun to catch attractive character lines about her eyes and mouth and there was an air of quiet dignity and self containment about her that Caroline always envied.

'I've got him over here in the shade,' Steven said, slipping his hand in hers and pulling her with him, 'but I don't know if he'd rather be in the sun. What do you think?'

She lifted her shoulders, stopping near a massive boulder on the cliff path. 'I don't really know much about snakes,' she said. 'Tim would, though. Shall I ask him when he gets home from school? Or better still,' she grinned, 'why not come home with me and ask him yourself?'

'Could I?'

'I'm sure Morwenna wouldn't mind. In fact, that's one of the reasons I came today. I'd like to have you and her and your dad come for dinner. You could come early and help me set the table. Would you like that?' Her grin turned rueful when she thought of the way Sharon had been badgering her all week to ask David to dinner. Grandy was exasperated by the way she always managed to find some excuse to put herself in David's proximity, interfering with his work. He tried to put a stop to it by giving her extra chores to keep her busy in the house but Sharon wasn't about to let that defeat her.

'Oh, yes!' Steven's eyes shone. 'When Sharon came to bring us some eggs last night, she told me you have a dog. And she said I'd like Tim. We're on the same wave length.'

She looked at the thin green snake coiled in the box and gave a relieved laugh. 'Sharon's right. You are a lot alike. Tim's got a snake who's probably this one's brother.' She only hoped Steven wasn't the type who liked putting them down the back of a girl's shirt the way Tim did when he thought things were too quiet around the house.

Something flashed in Steven's eyes when he gingerly picked up his snake. He hesitated only a moment but it was enough of a warning for Caroline.

'Don't do it,' she said softly. 'Don't even think it.'

His eyes danced. 'What?' he said innocently enough.

'I'll . . . I'll . . .' She swallowed and began to back away but tripped on a rock and landed in a sitting position in the middle of the path.

The snake slithered down the front of her blouse and she gave a yelp, furiously twisting and turning, fumbling with her buttons, trying to let him loose. 'Oh, Steven, I'll get you for this!'

He doubled over, laughing so hard there were tears in his eyes. He was practically rolling on the ground.

Caroline whimpered in frustration, tearing off a button before finally getting rid of the snake. Once it was safely back in its box, she advanced on him.

'I couldn't help it,' he gurgled.

'Oh, couldn't you?' She caught his shoulders with mock gruffness as if she was going to shake the life out of him but then she gathered his thin little body in her arms and hugged him instead. 'I should have been warned, shouldn't I? When you said you and Tim were on the same wave length.'

He laughed and burrowed his face deeper into her softness, the gesture coming as naturally as breathing. 'Sharon told me how Tim was always teasing you like that. I wanted to try it as well.'

She expelled her breath loudly to let him know what she thought of that. 'Am I to expect this sort of thing from now on, when the both of you get together?'

'Oh no,' he said at once, drawing away from her, his face solemn again. 'You weren't really scared, were you?'

'And if I was?'

'I won't do it again. I promise.'

'Well, I wasn't scared. I just don't like them in my shirt.' She glanced sideways at him and saw the devilish grin begin again. 'Or in my jeans, either,' she said quickly. 'So get rid of that idea right now. Next time, if there is a next time, you won't get off so lightly.'

His grin was infectious and they went back

to the garden hand in hand, an invisible bond running from his heart to hers.

Little shafts of sunlight dappled the ground under the gnarled apple tree sprinkling her with shadowy comfort. The warm breeze sighed over the rugged boulders tumbling down the cliffs to the sea as sea gulls dipped and wheeled overhead. Caroline sipped her tea and smiled in contentment, loving this place more each time she came. Steven was playing with Morwenna's grey and white cat on the grass a little way away from them.

'It's so restful here,' Caroline said softly. 'I almost envy you this house, Morwenna. Every time I come, I can feel my batteries getting recharged.'

Her friend chuckled. 'You surprise me. I would have thought it would take more than a peaceful afternoon in a cliffside garden to make you happy. Sharon's batteries got a high voltage jolt when David came to work for you.'

'Yes, well,' her lips twisted, 'Sharon hasn't learned discretion yet. She's really crazy about him and make no bones about it. Sometimes I think the way she acts must embarrass him.'

'How do you feel about him? For the past week Sharon's come round every day to get me to tell her everything I know about him. Would you mind having David for a brother-in-law?'

She squirmed uncomfortably, feeling a telltale blush creep up her neck. How could she answer that truthfully? Her thoughts were so jumbled lately. David was good and kind to Grandy and the boys and especially gentle with her father. He worked hard around the farm but she didn't really know if she wanted to see him married to Sharon. All her brothers did. At least they said so often enough this past week. But David didn't seem to be overly interested in Sharon and for some strange reason that made her feel . . . relieved.

'Don't you think you're being a bit premature?' she hedged. 'Sharon's out to hook him but so far David's not even nibbling at her bait.'

'Nicely put,' Morwenna grinned. 'Just between you and me, he's not the man for her.'

'But she loves him. You know she does. I think it's only a matter of time before he realises it and begins to love her back.'

'Let's see . . .' Morwenna pursed her lips. 'She loved John Polgearon last month and Alan Penrhyn the month before that . . . and wasn't there someone named Simon something or other . . .?' her voice trailed off as if she didn't really have to go on.

'This is different. She knew David before. Look what she did to make sure he'd notice her again.'

'You mean that horrid dye job? Give the man credit for having more brains than that. He wouldn't be flattered if he knew. He needs a quiet kind of love—from someone level headed, who has both feet on the ground, who'll fill the empty places in his heart and be a good mother to his son and all the other children he's meant to have.'

'Meant to have? That's a curious thing to say. Did he tell you that?'

'No, silly. Haven't you ever taken a good look at him? It's written all over him. That man's made to be a father to a large family.'

Caroline smiled innocently enough but her heart began to thump unsteadily. To be the woman he chose for his wife, to have the right to work at his side and share all the intimacies of love and passion with him, to be the mother of his beautiful children. The mere thought took her breath away. And then she shook herself. What was the matter with her? She had dreamed these dreams before, in Philip's arms, and they had all been shattered. She wouldn't begin them again. Not with a man as far out of reach as David. It was doomed to failure before it even began.

'David knows the loneliness of being an only child,' Morwenna said softly, 'and so did Judith. He doesn't want Steven to grow up like that.'

'Sharon's flighty,' she said with a sinking

feeling she couldn't explain, 'but she'd be a good mother.'

'She's not for him!' Morwenna was emphatic and her dark eyes flashed.

'Don't be too sure. She's out to get him. That's one of the reasons I came today. To invite you and David and Steven to dinner tonight. Will you come?'

'Do I have a choice?'

Her face fell. 'Don't you *want* to come?'

'Not if I have to watch you let Sharon make a fool of herself over David.'

'Morwenna——'

'All right, all right,' she sighed. 'I won't go on about it. But I could shake you, Caroline. One of these days you're going to pull your head out of the sand and stop giving priority to self-protection. You're going to allow yourself to experience and express loving emotions again and you'll see what's staring you in the face.'

'I can see it already. When you love someone, you give them power over you. Love is for fools who are afraid to be their own person.'

Morwenna shook her head and sighed and decided to change the subject instead of arguing. She knew Caroline could be as stubborn as a mule when she wanted to be. 'How's your father today?'

A frown creased her forehead and she lifted her shoulders helplessly. 'Funny you should ask that. All this past week I've noticed a look on his face but I can't explain it. It's not exactly pain but when he looks at David, I know he sees him and knows who he is. It's almost as if Daddy wants to offer him—sympathy. Isn't that crazy? Grandy says I'm imagining things.'

Morwenna leaned towards her. 'Give me your hand.'

'Oh, come on.'

'No, no, I'm not going to read your palm. Just let me see.' She took first one hand, then the other and searched them. 'See that line there? The one running from the middle of your wrist straight up to your middle finger?'

Caroline looked and nodded. Morwenna had it on both her hands too.

'They say people who have that mark are somewhat psychic.' She sat back in her chair and smiled an intriguing smile. 'Perhaps you're not imagining things at all. Perhaps your father knows something none of the rest of us know about David and that's why he's sympathetic. I always thought you were more sensitive than most. Who knows? Maybe with a little practice you'll find you have the gift of a sixth sense.'

'Heaven forbid!'

'Oh, it's not so bad. Sometimes it's even a blessing.'

She looked sceptical.

'Not all the time, I'll grant you. Like when

there's something unfortunate about to happen and you know you can't do anything to change it.' A troubled frown crossed her face. 'It makes you restless and kind of jumpy. Unsettled.'

Caroline tilted her head. 'That's the way you've been for the past half hour. Oh yes,' she said quickly at Morwenna's look of surprise. 'I know you're been trying to hide it but I noticed it right away, as soon as I came up the path. Don't tell me you're picking up some bad vibrations from somewhere?'

'I knew you were sensitive. You're right. Something is wrong.' She gripped her hands nervously together in her lap and bit her lip and looked beyond her. 'I'm afraid we'll know what it is all too soon. Here comes David.'

Caroline wheeled around and was on her feet at once, unconsciously holding her breath. He was supposed to be overhauling the tractor with Grandy this afternoon.

David's quiet approach was deceptive. Coming from the side of the cottage, his long fluid strides ate up the distance between them in no time at all. He came straight to Caroline and searched her face for one timeless instant without saying anything.

Her eyes widened and became full of mute pleading.

'It's your grandfather,' he said, his mouth shaking. 'I think he's had a stroke.'

CHAPTER THREE

SHATTERED, Caroline could only look at him. Grandy? A stroke? No! Nothing could touch him. He'd never been sick a day in his life, not even a cold. When her whole world ended last year, he was the one who kept her from falling apart by going on with his abrasive, no-nonsense, everyday routine. It hadn't changed in all his sixty-five years. It couldn't change now. He was tall and spare, a man of the earth. Nothing bothered Grandy. It couldn't be a stroke. That only happened to people who were over-weight and who smoked and who had high blood pressure. None of those things described him. Grandy was healthy.

Or was he? Her thoughts screeched to a halt then began rushing in another direction. Maybe he'd been failing all along and just never said anything. Maybe that was why he was so insistent on hiring a housekeeper and someone to help him with the farmwork, only he was too proud to tell her the real reason. Oh, Grandy! Why hadn't he trusted her enough? She trembled. Each of them in his own way had leaned on him and now she realised how selfish that was. She drained his strength when she should have been lending him some of hers. He was always there when she needed him. She'd have to be there for him now.

A small sob rose in her throat as the mist cleared from her eyes. She felt David's hands on her shoulders. He was looking straight into her face with eyes that unnerved her. She had never seen them this close before. They were brilliantly blue and full of a calm quiet strength he was more than willing to share with her. Her legs were curiously weak and shaking as panic tried to claw at the edges of her mind. This wasn't the same as when they came and told her her mother was dead in a road accident. David was here now, shielding her from the pain.

He gently drew her into the warm secure circle of his arms. It was safe here. She had nothing to fear. Nothing could touch her. Just for a minute she buried her face in his chest, breathing in the warm earthy scent of him.

He was sweating and had spent his time with the cows this morning but Caroline could only smell the fresh clean scent of the sun and the wind and the sea that was uniquely his. Her arms curled around his broad back as if she had every right to embrace him. He was warm and solid against her palms, his length fitting so perfectly against hers. She wished she never had to let him go.

For a long minute he simply held her, his chin resting on the top of her head, then with obvious reluctance, he gently loosened his hold, his hands slipping down her arms to support her trembling body. Before he released her completely and stepped away, she caught a fleeting look of something in his eyes but she had no idea what it was.

'Where is Grandy now?' Morwenna asked softly, her face full of concern.

'On his way to hospital. John Polgearon was with us when he collapsed. He took Grandy in his car. I left Sharon with her father and came for Caroline.'

'You were right to do that. If Grandy needs anybody now, it's Caro.' Her husky voice suddenly became brisk when she noticed her standing there so stricken. 'Go with David,' she said. 'Steven and I will see to your father and the boys when they come home from school. We'll wait for you there.'

Caroline nodded dumbly. So many things were trying to crowd in on her. She couldn't makc sense out of any of them. Her legs were like rubber when she tried to move forward. All she had to do was put one foot in front of the other but her legs refused to move.

David reached out and gently linked her hands with his, letting his strength flow into her cold shaking fingers. Then he touched her cheek. 'I'm here,' he said gently.

A convulsive shudder trembled through

her. Nothing could happen to Grandy. David was here to make everything all right. A travesty of a smile pulled at her mouth when she looked blindly up at him. 'Yes,' she whispered through the tight ball of pain in her throat.

His strong arm curved around her back, guiding her to his car. In reality, he half-carried her there.

Everything flashed by in a blur on their way to the hospital in Penzance. A stiff breeze was blowing through the open window but it didn't cool her churning emotions. It was a warm afternoon with the sunlight glittering on the tossing blue expanse of Mount's Bay as they streaked along the road. Seagulls wheeled in the distance and the water foamed against the rocks.

Can't this car go any faster? she thought, her hands trembling in her lap.

A smile loosened the tense muscles of David's jaw. 'We're flying low as it is.'

She froze, her gaze clashing with his. How could he know what she was thinking? She hadn't said a word out loud.

As if in answer, he simply reached out and curled one big hand around both of hers and squeezed. The pressure was pleasurably firm and comforting and she found an enveloping warmth creeping up her arms and flowing to the rest of her. At once her anxiety lessened. He was a man of few words and somehow it was right that he didn't need them. She knew if it was at all possible he would make everything all right.

The hands of the clock dragged interminably in the hospital waiting room. John Polgearon had to leave after waiting with them for more than an hour. David promised to let him know as soon as they had something to report. Caroline jerkily paced the floor, tensing every time someone walked past the door. This isn't the same as when Mum died, she kept telling herself. Her head was throbbing and she roughly rubbed her temples with her fingertips before finally subsiding on to a chair. Surely somebody ought to know something by now?

David sat across the room from her, silent and unmoving, yet she knew this must be hard for him as well. It must bring back memories of the hours he spent in hospital waiting while Judith slowly died of cancer. Her heart went out to him. How could he sit there so calmly?

His hair was windblown, a stray light brown lock falling across his forehead. No matter how many times he pushed it back, it kept falling into his eyes until he finally left it there. The calm strength she noticed before was still in his eyes. They were a darker blue now and compelling. His nose had a slight bump on the bridge of it as if it had been broken at some time. Deep craggy lines of time and experience were etched on the sides of his mouth. Like brackets, she thought, cleaving his strong jaw, enclosing the fluid line of his lips. His chin had a faint cleft in the middle of it. She followed the movement of his neck when he swallowed.

A pale blue shirt stretched across his flatly muscled chest with sleeves rolled back to his elbows exposing strong arms tanned and sprinkled with glinting blonde hairs. His jeans were faded and worn soft, hugging his long legs as they stretched out in front of him and crossed at the ankles. His boots were a dusty dark brown and she wondered how far and what kind and how many places they had taken him.

She never gave much thought to her own appearance before. Sharon was the beauty of the family. Caroline was plain and took it for granted. Tall and gangly with long brown hair usually falling down her back in a single braid, she was suddenly conscious of her plainness and how disheveled she must look to him. Her white blouse was clean but wrinkled and had a button missing where she had torn it earlier. Her jeans were old and stained. Canvas shoes, no longer white, were on her feet.

Her eyes returned to his steady gaze seeing something stir in those dark blue depths before she abruptly turned away. Warmth flooded her body. She had been caught staring and somehow he knew exactly what she was thinking. She marvelled that he could walk around in her mind like that.

Just then a white-haired man with a stethoscope around his neck came in and David was forgotten. She jumped to her feet and held her breath.

'Miss Pentreath?'

She nodded jerkily, her eyes widening.

His face was bland. 'I'm Doctor Treveglos. Your grandfather's had a stroke,' he said quietly. 'He's resting comfortably at the moment. Will you come to my office where we can talk further?'

At once David was beside her, his arm tightening around her shoulders to give her the strength to follow him.

'Your grandfather's a very lucky man,' the doctor said dispassionately, motioning for them to sit down. 'It was a relatively slight stroke. Just enough to shake him up a bit. I've been warning him this might happen if he didn't slow down.'

Caroline let out a gasping breath, unaware until now that she had been holding it. 'I didn't know.' She subsided awkwardly in her chair, staring at him. 'He never said anything.'

'Evidently Mr Pentreath's been seeing you for some time, Doctor,' David's quiet voice came between them, soothing her raw nerves. 'Has he been having problems long?'

'He's had a rheumatic heart condition for years but we've been able to keep it under control. For the past year, however,' he glanced at the chart in front of him, 'he's been under a great deal of stress with—his son?' He raised his eyebrows and looked at Caroline over the rims of his glasses. 'Your father?'

She nodded unhappily, twisting her fingers together. She thought she had done so well caring for all of them, but all this time Grandy was worrying himself right into a stroke. 'He never said anything!' she almost cried, sudden guilt and anger and dismay running across her face.

David's strong fingers closed over hers, stilling her fears. His calm eyes probed hers with disturbing intensity. 'You must know he wouldn't have wanted to burden you with it. You were already doing the best you could do.'

She shuddered, remembering how only last week Grandy said her best wasn't good enough.

His face softened with compassion, as if he knew, then he looked back to the doctor, taking charge without taking over. 'What can we do?'

The older man visibly relaxed in the face of this calm acceptance of the inevitable.

'Very little at the moment. Mr Pentreath's vision is affected in one eye and his speech is hesitant. There's some paralysis on his right side as well. He's being given medication to stabilise him and we'll begin therapy later today. I see no reason why we can't expect a complete recovery in a matter of months. The main thing is to keep him calm and free from anxiety.'

Caroline compressed her lips wondering how that was possible. Nothing had changed. When he came home, her father would still be the same. She'd still be his jilted granddaughter, the inadequate substitute for her mother, the cause of all his problems. 'May I see him?' she asked.

He regarded her intently. 'Can you go in there and reassure him? Make him believe he has nothing to worry about?'

'We will,' David cut in forcefully, not looking at her.

Strangely enough she knew it just might be possible. There was something about David that inspired confidence. Maybe something would work out after all. She nodded to the doctor and smiled tremulously. 'Yes, we will,' she echoed.

Grandy looked frail against the white sheets in the high hospital bed. His face was grey and his workworn hands looked oddly pale lying there so flaccidly at his sides. Caroline's bottom lip quivered but somehow she managed to smile. 'Oh, Grandy,' she whispered.

One side of his face was twisted and a small muscle was jerking in his jaw when his eyes fluttered open and he tried to speak. Harsh unintelligible sounds came from his throat. His good hand clenched and his eyes strained angrily.

'It's all right,' David soothed, gripping his hand hard. Leaning closer, he gave him an eloquent wordless look, willing away his fears. 'You don't have to say a thing. Just rest. Morwenna and I will stay with your family until you're well again. The doctor said your stroke was slight. You'll be up and around in no time. Do you believe me?'

Grandy stared at him for a minute then his eyes suddenly filled with tears.

'Believe me!' David said fiercely. 'I wouldn't lie to you! Nothing will happen to any of you. I won't let it!' He made himself smile more gently and curled his free arm around Caroline, moulding her close to his side. 'This is a good woman you've got here. Between us we'll keep everything under control.'

Grandy's eyes flared then flickered closed and he relaxed, falling deeply asleep, a faint smile softening his lips.

Caroline trembled, wondering how David could project such calm assurance like that. He barely knew them, after all. How could

Grandy trust him so completely? It wasn't right. Every instinct told her it wasn't right.

She stiffened suddenly and pulled away from him, some strange compulsion telling her she was crazy to trust him. That was the first step. First came trust, then love, then betrayal.

David's mouth twisted and with a curt nod, he motioned that it was time to leave. 'We'll let him sleep. That's the best thing right now.'

Once in the hallway, she sagged against the wall. 'He looks so awful!'

'You should have seen him when he collapsed a few hours ago!'

The harshness in David's voice jerked her head up. He had been so calm, so gentle before. She almost didn't recognise him as the same man of only a moment ago. His face was rigid and cold and stern, as if he was controlling some fierce inner anger.

And then it dawned on her and something inside began to shrivel. All this time it was an act! A grand gesture! He wasn't the strong silent one totally in control, taking on the responsibility of their well being. He was a stranger suddenly trapped into helping them, dragged in because he happened to be there when Grandy needed someone and now because of some mad impulse on his part, he was being forced to keep on helping. They were nothing to him and it was wrong to impose on him like this. She had two perfectly good feet. It was time to stand on them all by herself.

Something stiffened inside her and she stepped away from the wall, straightening her shoulders, her chin coming up with stubborn pride. Smoothing her shaking hands down the sides of her jeans, she bunched them into fists to steady them and gave him a bright smile to hide her painfully evident distress. 'Thank you for all your help, David. I . . .' she swallowed past a dry lump in her throat, '. . . appreciate all you've done. If there's some way I can repay——'

'Oh, stop!' he cut in harshly. 'I have to make a 'phone call. I'll meet you outside in a few minutes.' He strode away without another word or a backward glance.

When he brought the car around, Caroline was still reeling from his harshness. He could have accepted her thanks. It was all she had to give. Her teeth were clenched so tightly they hurt but she got in the front seat without a word, her thoughts racing.

How could she be so stupid? David was a stranger. She could have died of embarrassment when she remembered how willingly she went into his arms earlier. As if she belonged there! As if he could make everything all right! Was he going to think . . .? She shuddered. She didn't want to know what he thought.

By degrees the silence between them became frigid. The sun was sinking into the bay with a brilliant rosy splash as they drove home. Caroline barely noticed. She was only conscious of the sharp line of David's profile, all stony and hard. He ignored her, his eyes staying on the road, his mouth a thin bluish line.

She felt sick with self-recrimination. The air was heavy and oppressive and her throat ached with the sudden need to cry. Her chin quivered and she blinked furiously at the hot tears rising in her eyes. This had to stop. Men hated tears. If he saw, it would only bring more and greater humiliation down on her head.

The motor stopped humming and she pulled herself together, looking around uninterestedly. They weren't even near home yet. David had left the motorway for a little used lane ending in a cove and was thrusting open his door and getting out as if he couldn't stand to be near her any more. She watched him walk to the edge of a low cliff with its boulders tumbling headlong into the sea. His hands were shoved deep in his pockets and he was staring moodily at the swirling water below.

It was deserted here, the bracken thick and blowing. Dusk was rapidly falling and Caroline got out and breathed deeply, trying to get things back into perspective. The future never looked so bleak but somehow she'd survive. Somehow she'd do it. Scrambling down the rocks closer to the water, she told herself it wasn't the end of the world. She was capable of taking care of herself and her family without asking any favours from anyone.

A stiff breeze struck at her, loosening her hair from her thick braid and she had to drag it out of her eyes to keep herself upright. Reaching some loose, shifting sand and rock, her feet shot out from under her and she pitched forward, tumbling almost into the water, sprawling flat on her face in a shower of sharp wet gravel. In a way she was glad. It gave her a reason for the uncontrollable tears that began to trickle down her face.

There was the sound of more loose gravel still falling behind her, then: 'What are you trying to do? Break your bloody neck?' David bit out violently, hurtling down the cliff. Falling to his knees, he lifted her by the shoulders and turned her roughly on her back.

'Well if I am, it's *my* bloody neck!' she sobbed. Tears were streaming from her eyes and her nose was running and there wasn't a thing she could do about it. 'Go away and leave me alone. I don't need you!'

His hands tightened, hurting her, digging into her shoulders. 'You selfish little fool! That's what this is all about, isn't it? All of a sudden you realised just how much you do need me. I saw it in your eyes when you looked at your grandfather. And then you had to pull away from me, didn't you? You couldn't let me help you.' His voice shook with jeering contempt. 'Oh no, not Caroline. She doesn't need anybody. Nobody gets close to her. That might mean leaving herself wide open to hurt again. Damn you, Caroline! Do you think I'd ever hurt you?'

Her eyes widened and she glared at him in this half light. How could he know that? How *dare* he know her better than she knew herself? If there were times when she was strangely restless and felt a painful sense of emptiness, she never let herself dwell on it. If she deliberately stayed away from people and cared for her family, it wasn't because she was afraid of needing someone and being hurt again. That wasn't it at all. He was wrong. He had to be wrong.

She quivered, wanting to voice her resentment, but she couldn't utter a sound. The sudden shimmer of pain in his eyes caught her and held. He knew everything and understood and wanted to help her.

An abrupt stillness came between them, a breathless suspended moment needing no words. They kept looking at each other and neither of them dared to breathe.

Her eyes probed his for one more long second before his face came closer, his eyes closing before his mouth came down on hers. It was inevitable, unfathomable, but not the least bit hesitant. She never would have believed anything so gentle could be so masterful. If he had demanded a response, she wouldn't have given him one. But he drank from her lips as if from a fragile vessel and everything inside her melted.

Yielding, pliant, she lay on the sharp stones feeling only the warm touch of his lips on hers, the silken strength of his hands sliding up her shoulders to cup her neck, his fingers disappearing into the tangled thickness of her hair.

He wasn't taking a thing. He was giving.

Her arms came up and settled on his broad back, the wild leap of her heart quickening and flooding with a bruising sweet rush of desire. Instinctively her mouth opened like a flower and she was lost in a devastating surge of feeling she never knew was possible.

His breath filled her. He was giving so much. The well was endless. He kept on giving.

Philip had kissed her many times but never like this, never ever with this soul-stirring gentleness. For the first time since she had been left waiting at the church, hope flared. The ice surrounding her heart began to move.

David had been kneeling beside her but at some point he must have shifted his position.

She became conscious of the entire length of his warm heavy body against hers and delighted in the exquisiteness of being so close to him. It was glorious and reassuring and somehow so right. If only she could stay with him forever. If only she had the right to lie with him and love him in all the ways there were . . .

Her eyes flew open.

It couldn't last. He was giving her so much and she had nothing to give in return. He didn't want her gratitude yet she couldn't give him anything else. To draw from his strength the way she had done to Grandy would make her a taker and she would never be that. It went against every principle she believed in.

Everything stopped. David sighed as if he knew where her thoughts were taking her and gently eased himself away from her. Sitting up, he dragged his hands through his hair. After a moment he got to his feet and stood looking down at her, something suspiciously like anger running across his face before it settled into impassive lines. Then he carefully lifted her to her feet.

'You're not taking advantage of me by accepting my help,' he said huskily, brushing down his jeans. 'I wouldn't have offered if I hadn't wanted to do it.'

'It's wrong, David. It's an imposition.' Her voice shook and she hunched her shoulders.

'I don't want to argue with you.' He kept

his voice gentle with an effort. 'And I'm not going to apologise for what just happened either. I wanted to do it and we both enjoyed it, though I'm sure you'd be the last to admit it. Everybody needs somebody, Caroline. You're not alone any more whether you want it that way or not.'

CHAPTER FOUR

WHEN they reached home Caroline blocked it all out of her mind. There were sure to be more pressing problems waiting for her. Expecting to find her family in utter chaos, she was surprised to see them at the kitchen table quietly finishing up their evening meal.

Her brothers sat in their places slightly subdued and nervously glancing at Morwenna as if she were some kind of stern fairy godmother who loved them but would put up with no nonsense.

Morwenna sat in Caroline's place at the foot of the table speaking brightly to their father as if there wasn't a thing wrong with him. 'I've forgotten, Alec. Do you take sugar in your coffee?' she asked.

When he kept staring emptily ahead without answering, she shrugged in an offhand way.

'I don't use it myself,' she went on. 'Bad for the figure at our age. I suppose you feel the same?' She knew as well as anyone that he preferred two spoonsful but she deftly moved the sugar bowl out of his reach. If he wanted it, he'd have to ask or help himself.

Sharon opened her mouth but at an almost

imperceptible flick of Morwenna's wrist, she stopped and sat back without saying anything.

'Ah, Caro. David.' Morwenna smiled at them and gracefully rose from her chair. 'You're back just in time. I've left your plates warming in the oven but you look as if you could do with a good cup of tea first.'

'Coffee,' David said abruptly.

That brought Morwenna's head up with a jerk. She never heard him speak harshly before. Her eyes immediately went from his to Caroline's strained face before narrowing thoughtfully. 'Coffee, then,' she smiled.

'Oh, David!' Sharon launched herself into his arms, clinging tightly.

Watching his arms instinctively close around her, a cold hand twisted Caroline's stomach, bringing with it a sudden flood of guilt. Her mouth began to throb with the memory of his kiss and she unthinkingly put up her hand as if to cover an imprint he'd left behind. Why hadn't she given a thought to Sharon? For a week now Sharon had been sending out all kinds of blatant signals that she found David fascinating and attractive and hoped eventually to make him hers.

Caroline turned at once, afraid that everything she felt was written all over her face. She started to leave the kitchen when Tim rushed up to her, wrapping his arms around her thighs. She couldn't very well push him away. Her own problems would have to wait. Gently releasing his hold, she went down on her knees beside him, letting him press his face into her neck. 'It's all right, Tim,' she soothed, knowing he didn't really understand any of this. 'Grandy's going to be all right.'

'David rang and told us that but Robbie said he was going to die! Just like Mum did! Just like Steven's Mum, too!' His eyes filled with tears and he sobbed into her neck.

'Oh he did, did he?' She threw Rob an impatient look.

He sat at the table next to Michael, red faced and belligerent. 'Well, he might. How do you know he won't?'

Tim drew away from her to look into her face with tear-drenched eyes, wanting to be reassured but too full of doubts to really trust her.

'No one can say for sure when someone is or isn't going to die,' she said truthfully, wanting to shake Rob until his teeth rattled. Tim was no stranger to death but he didn't need his brother hurling it at him again so cruelly like this. 'When we left Grandy, he was sleeping peacefully. The doctor told us,' her voice began to quiver, 'the stroke he had was slight. With medication and therapy there's no reason for him not to be fine again in a few months.'

Tim searched her face. 'If that's the truth,

then why are your eyes all red? You've been crying too.'

'Of course she has,' David said quietly, untangling himself from Sharon and coming down on his haunches beside them. Drawing Steven to one side and Tim away from Caroline to the other, he curled an arm around each of them and smiled reassuringly. 'She was just as scared as you were until the doctor came and told us Grandy was going to be all right. Then she fell apart.' He gave Tim a conspiratorial smile and winked as if he was imparting some strictly male wisdom. 'Women! How can we ever understand them? *We* cry when we think something's wrong—not when we find out it's all right.'

At once Tim relaxed against him and even managed a watery grin before scrubbing away his tears. 'Yeah, women!' he said scathingly. 'Grandy always says he can't understand Caro because she's half a bubble off plumb.'

David's jaw quivered and he tried to keep his grin contained but he couldn't quite manage it. He threw his head back and practically roared with helpless laughter. Caroline coloured hotly. She hadn't heard that one before. The rest of her brothers joined in and even Morwenna had to smile. Her father stared ahead unblinkingly and Sharon just stood and watched David with a dreamy look on her face.

'What's plumb, Daddy?' Steven's little voice floated up to him.

He kept chuckling. 'It's a weight suspended from the end of a line. It's used to determine whether something's straight.'

Steven frowned, not getting the connection.

'You know that level I have in my tool box? The one with the bubble that floats in the little glass tube?' he explained patiently—to Caroline's annoyance. Why didn't he just forget it?

Steven nodded.

'Well, when you measure something and it's not quite level, the bubble isn't in the centre. It's said to be off plumb.' He flashed Caroline a devilish grin, hugely enjoying himself at her expense. 'Half a bubble off plumb means she's not quite right.'

Steven looked from him to her, not smiling at all. Then he gravely reached out and put a comforting hand on her shoulder. 'I think your bubbles are all in the right places,' he said gently.

She felt an inexplicable tightness gather in her throat but she flashed a smug look to all of them and hugged her champion tightly. 'Thank you, kind sir. How very gallant of you to say so.'

David became unusually still, looking at his son artlessly wrapped in her arms. Then his eyes met hers and something moved in them.

'All right, all of you, the joke's over,' Morwenna said briskly, shattering the moment. 'Time to get busy. Rob, will you help Sharon sort out the bedrooms? We need two extra. One for David and one for me. Steven can bunk with Tim . . .' she quirked a dark eyebrow at Tim, '. . . that is, if there are no shenanigans at bedtime. Mike, take Tim and Steven with you to make sure the cows are in for the night—or out—or whatever it is you do with them.' Her no-nonsense voice had them all scattering at once. 'Caroline, you and David come and sit down. I'll have your meal on the table in no time.' Her eyes flicked to their father, surreptitiously reaching for the sugar bowl. A smile ran across her lips but she pretended not to see. 'I realise you had to be brief on the telephone, David. Now you can fill Alec and me in on all the details . . .'

Everything seemed to be working out fine, Caroline reflected later that night as she lay in her room under the eaves, staring at the ceiling in the dark. Morwenna had everything under control Her father was being looked after. The boys were all settled and knew what was expected of them. David was capable of handling the farmwork with her brothers' sporadic help. Tomorrow she and Sharon would start daily visits to the hospital to see Grandy. So why was she feeling so tearful and strangely bereft?

Everything was falling into place with no effort on Morwenna's part, that was why. It should have eased her mind. Instead, it only made her more aware of her own inadequacies. In the past year nothing ran this smoothly for her.

David was the fly in the ointment, she thought resentfully. He kept insinuating himself into everything. No matter how much she tried to banish him from her thoughts, he wouldn't leave.

She punched her pillow and turned on her side, resolutely closing her eyes, trying to quiet her troubled conscience. 'I won't think about him,' she whispered, her throbbing body aware that he was only a few feet down the hall from her. It was ridiculous. He meant nothing to her. He belonged to Sharon. If only she'd never said hello . . .

Everything that happened on their way home this evening kept weaving its way through her mind with frightening intensity. It wasn't the first time she'd ever been kissed so why was she making such a big deal of it? But there it was: the blueness of his eyes, the pleasurably rough texture of his skin, the thick silkiness of his hair sliding through her fingers, the muscled hardness of his body warmly pressing against the entire length of hers, the infinite gentleness of his mouth . . .

She despised herself for remembering it all so vividly.

Sharon would be devastated if she knew. David belonged to Sharon, she argued with herself. Sharon was closer in age as well as interests. Ten years stood between Caroline and David. Ten years of age and wisdom and experience. It was too much of a difference. She could never hope to bridge the gap. Sharon, maybe, but not Caroline.

She was plain. He was handsome. She fell apart in emergencies. He remained quietly in control. She had never travelled out of Cornwall. He had been as far away as America. She knew nothing at all about life or love or happiness. He knew everything about all of them. He had lived, loved, married. He even had a son.

She tossed and turned, kicked off the sheet, pulled it up again, smoothed her white cotton nightgown with shaking fingers, scrubbed her hands across her face. Oh, what was the matter with her? She turned on her back and grimaced in the dark.

Grandy would soon be better and when he came home, David would go back to Morwenna's, she told herself. She'd be left in peace. She turned on her other side and gripped her pillow with a clenched fist. No she wouldn't. He'd end up marrying Sharon and she'd spend all her time imagining them together.

She could see his tall powerful body curled into Sharon's warm curves, his hands ruffling her black wisps of hair, his arms enfolding her in that charmed circle . . .

She sat up with a jerk. No! She buried her face in her hands, willing away this insanity. She wouldn't be jealous. Sharon was welcome to him. She didn't want him, she thought desperately. She didn't want any man. She wouldn't love again. Love meant emptiness and loss and betrayal. She wouldn't let it happen again, David was nothing! Sharon would be good to him. Let her try her luck with men. Caroline was through. She had her father and her brothers. They were enough. They had to be enough.

And then she remembered David's gently mocking voice. '*. . . oh no, not Caroline, she doesn't need anybody . . . that might mean leaving herself wide open to hurt again . . . damn you . . . do you think I'd ever hurt you?*'

I don't know, she thought. I don't want to find out. If only she hadn't said hello.

Caroline was late for breakfast the next morning. They were just finishing when she came in with mumbled apologies. No one commented on her puffy eyes or wan appearance. They all knew how attached she was to Grandy and how worried she had been. It was only natural she'd have a hard time getting to sleep last night.

Her heart missed a beat when she looked at

David but she turned her head sharply and studiously avoided looking at him sitting at the opposite end of the table. His features were taut and a muscle jerked in his cheek. She had a feeling he was as aware of her as she was of him.

Morwenna's eyes became thoughtful but nothing was said.

Later in the morning when the housework was done and she and Morwenna were alone in the kitchen preparing lunch, Caroline thanked her for seeing to her father earlier.

'I usually get up a few minutes early to shave him,' she said softly. 'I don't know how I could oversleep like that.'

Morwenna stopped peeling potatoes and looked up, astounded. 'You shave him!' she choked, her hands curling around the edge of the sink.

'Why, yes.' Her face fell. 'Didn't you do it for him this morning? I noticed how smooth his face looked.'

'*Caroline!*'

She hunched her shoulders.

'I don't believe it! You actually shave your father?' Her mouth fell open in shock.

'Ever since—Philip,' she stopped and gripped her arms together almost hugging her waist. 'He was letting himself go, Morwenna. And it was all my fault. Naturally I had to take care of him.'

'Oh, naturally,' she said scathingly.

Caroline looked at her in helpless confusion. 'You should have seen him,' she defended herself. 'He looked so scruffy. His beard was coming all patchy and shaggy-like.'

'Believe me, if it itched enough, he'd have shaved it off himself! Honestly, Caroline, I don't know where your head is sometimes. Shaving your father! And I suppose all this time you've been force-feeding him too? As if he were a baby?'

'Well—the way he is—it's all my fault.'

'Oh come on. It's nobody's fault. You've been carrying that burden of guilt long enough. It's time to put it behind you. I didn't shave your father this morning. I'm sure he wouldn't have thanked me if I'd tried. I'd probably have cut his face all up and made him bleed to death. As far as I know, he did it himself when you didn't show up to do it for him.'

Caroline's eyes widened.

'No wonder he never tried to bounce back! He didn't have to!' Morwenna's eyes flashed fire. 'Whatever happened between him and Philip Tregenna is best left in the past where it belongs. If your father had been able to put it behind him before now, he would have gone on and got better. But you never let him!' Her voice softened but she was angry too. 'You've got to stop doing everything for him, Caro. He's capable of caring for himself. If he gets hungry enough or thirsty enough, he'll get himself something to eat or drink. He's not a cripple but you're turning him into one.'

Caroline put a shaking hand to her mouth. 'I was only trying to help.'

'I know,' Morwenna said softly, suddenly contrite and full of sympathy. 'But sometimes you can try too hard and be too kind. Trust me, Caro. Your father's had some kind of shock so it'll take another one to bring him out of it. Maybe now's the time. Maybe this stroke of Grandy's is just the thing to turn everything around. All I ask is that you let me try to help him. Will you?'

She looked sceptical. 'What can you do?'

'I watched him last night and I have a plan. Just trust me,' she said again. 'and say nothing. No matter what. Understand?'

Caroline nodded uneasily, not really understanding at all.

At lunchtime, Morwenna sat in Caroline's place next to her father and watched Alec shuffle in and subside on to his chair with his vacant, preoccupied air. She spooned some fluffy mashed potatoes on to her plate then held out the bowl to him. 'Potatoes, Alec?' she asked quietly.

He stared ahead unseeingly.

Morwenna waited a minute then looked pointedly at his flat stomach. 'Well, you are getting a paunch, aren't you? At your age and with so little exercise it's inevitable. But total starvation to get rid of it is a bit drastic, don't you think? You didn't have any breakfast this morning. Surely you must be hungry?'

A dull red began to creep up his neck but he said nothing, staring emptily ahead as if he hadn't heard.

'Suit yourself,' she sighed, bypassing him and handing the bowl to Sharon with a bright smile.

Sharon's lips twitched and David grinned outright. An eloquent look passed between the two of them but they said nothing. Evidently Morwenna had already enlisted their help as well.

'Fried chicken, Alec?' she tried again.

At no response, the plate went to Sharon. His eyes flickered but still, he said nothing.

A green salad was next, followed by a big plate of spring vegetables.

They all sat quietly eating and it was all Caroline could do to keep herself from saying something. Her father looked so hungry. Morwenna knew this was one of his favourite meals. How could she be so cruel? But Caroline had promised, so she said nothing.

When they finished, Sharon began clearing the table. 'Coffee, Daddy?' she asked, her hand hovering near the coffee pot, wanting to pour some.

His eyes suddenly came alive, losing their

dull glazed expression. A look almost of triumph flashed to Morwenna but still he said nothing and his face didn't alter its lines of hopeless apathy. Only his eyes were alive.

When he didn't answer her, Sharon shrugged and took it to the sink and began pouring it down the drain.

Something like a sob broke the silence. He got to his feet and shuffled out, his gait more unsteady than usual.

Caroline's throat closed with tears. Ordinarily she had a great respect for Morwenna's wisdom but this time she didn't know what she was doing. 'You *can't* starve him, Morwenna!'

'Trust me,' she answered, turning away to hide a slightly worried frown. 'I knew he was a proud man. I just didn't realise he'd be this stubborn.'

'Where do you think Caroline gets it from?' David muttered, wadding up his napkin and pushing back his chair.

Bristling, Caroline opened her mouth to defend herself but out of the corner of her eye she saw Steven unobtrusively folding something in his napkin and stuffing it in his shirt.

He slid off his chair and followed her father out without a word.

As far as she knew, no one else noticed what he had done and not wanting to draw any attention to him, she dropped her eyes to her lap and kept silent.

A little later, before she left for the hospital with Sharon, she noticed her father sitting in the garden with Steven on the grass at his feet. She couldn't be sure but she thought she saw him wipe his mouth with the back of his hand and they both seemed to share the wary smiles of two conspirators.

CHAPTER FIVE

ALL the way to the hospital that day Sharon kept up a constant chatter until Caroline felt like screaming.

'Wasn't he just the most wonderful thing?' she asked for the umpteenth time. And for the umpteenth time didn't wait for an answer. 'The way he took right over! So big! So masterful! I knew there was nothing to worry about once he saw what was happening. He knew just what to do. You should have been there!'

Caroline ground the gears as they crawled along the winding leafy lanes fast becoming glutted with tourist traffic and gritted her teeth, wishing she could be anywhere else but in this car listening to her sister sing David's praises. She tried to concentrate on the sunshine shimmering in golden splashes on the bay at their side and the wildly beautiful rocky terrain but everything kept coming back to David.

She felt so guilty. It meant nothing, she told herself over and over. Some day he'd be her brother-in-law and he wouldn't thank her for remembering one stupid kiss given in a moment of compulsive sympathy.

She could picture herself through the years, watching him work in the fields, milking the cows, harvesting the grain, doing the hundred and one things needing to be done on the farm. And then when their bedroom door closed at night, Sharon would have him all to herself . . .

'Grandy fell off the tractor,' Sharon went on, oblivious to Caroline's distress. 'At first we thought he'd slipped but when we saw his face, we knew it had to be something else. Everything happened so fast after that.' Her smile became wistful. 'Oh, he was so wonderful. And to think, I almost let him get away! This time I'm going to marry him, Caro.'

Her lips compressed. 'Oh? Has he asked you?'

She laughed, undeterred by so inconsequential a thing. 'Not yet. But he will. It's only a matter of time. I remember thinking how strong he was when he lifted Grandy in his arms to put him in the car, and how lucky we were that he was there. It was providence that brought him back to me, wasn't it?'

'Providence,' she murmured, her mouth a trembling bitter line.

Why did he have to come back? Why couldn't he have stayed in America? Someone else would have been here to help Grandy. It didn't have to be David. If he hadn't come, she never would have had to see him again, seen what a gorgeous man he had become, or hear about him, or be plagued with his gentle insidious presence. Now he was everywhere. When she closed her eyes his face was there behind her lids. Her hands still quivered with the remembered feel of him; her nose, his scent; her ears, his voice; her mouth, the warm sweet invasion of his breath; her body, the glorious heaviness of his.

A small sob escaped her.

'Oh, Caro, don't worry!' Sharon reached over and squeezed her arm. 'David said Grandy's going to be all right. He knows what he's talking about. He wouldn't lie to us.'

Caroline nodded, pulling herself together with an effort, not correcting Sharon's mistaken assumption that she had been thinking about Grandy.

When they reached the hospital, Sharon's voice bubbled down the hushed corridor, greeting the doctor. They talked for a few minutes and suddenly Caroline was grateful for her sister's more outgoing personality. The doctor told her things he might not have mentioned to a more staid relative. He assured them Grandy was doing well and Sharon accepted it without question. Never feeling things too deeply, Sharon didn't make mountains out of molehills the way Caroline often did. Caroline could learn from her.

'Hello, Grandy,' Sharon said from the

doorway of his room, smiling brightly, missing the sudden clenching of his good hand as he looked at them.

'Grandy,' Caroline echoed softly behind her, missing nothing.

He looked a little better than yesterday but not much. Propped up on pillows, he looked pale. He was being fed through a vein in his hand and Caroline quickly looked away from the relentless drip of the clear liquid in the intravenous bottle and tried to smile.

'I see you're having pasties this afternoon,' Sharon said blithely, coming to the side of his bed and kissing him gently. 'The boys send their love and Morwenna says you're not to hurry and get well. She needs a little time to work on Daddy and if you're there, you'll only cramp her style.'

Caroline gasped at her offhand manner but a twisted smile softened Grandy's face.

'David?' he said slowly, having difficulty forming the words.

Sharon laughed delightedly. 'He's such a brick, Grandy!' The wistful look came back to her face, making Caroline's stomach plunge.

She turned away at once, pretending to straighten a box of tissues on the table at the side of the bed. 'David's got everything under control,' Caroline said in a wobbly voice. 'He's repairing the shed today and said to say hello.'

'I talked to John Polgearon this morning,' Sharon's voice was dreamy. 'He rang to find out how you were. He hoped the bumpy ride in his old car didn't jolt you too much or make you black and blue. He didn't know if you'd remember, but he said he broke all speed limits to get you here and he thought if you'd been able, you'd have yelled at him to slow down.'

Grandy actually chuckled at that and visibly relaxed.

It was so surprising and so welcome a sound that Caroline felt the prick of tears behind her eyes. 'Is there anything we can do for you?' she asked gently. 'Anything from home you'd like us to bring next time we come?'

He shook his head. 'I'll . . . go home . . . get it . . . myself . . .'

'We met the doctor in the corridor before we came in,' Sharon bubbled. 'He said you're the most exasperating patient he's ever had. You're much too independent!'

Caroline threw up her hands and rounded on her 'Sharon!'

'Well,' she hunched her shoulders, 'that's what he said.'

'I know, but you shouldn't tell Grandy that.'

'Why? Afraid it'll give him a swelled head?'

Caroline looked at her grandfather with helpless exasperation then stopped abruptly, drawing a sharp breath. Instead of becoming agitated, he was actually laughing in a self-satisfied way. Even his eyes danced.

Astonishment ran through her and a mixture of elation and chagrin. Sharon had known the right thing to say instinctively. Of course Grandy would want everyone to know he wasn't going to let this stroke stop him. Especially here. Especially now. It was exactly what he needed to hear. Why hadn't she known that? Something started to unravel deep inside her.

All this time she thought she was so great. *She* was the one with all the answers. *She* knew what was best for everybody. *She* was the little mother taking charge of all of them. Oh, the arrogance! It had taken this tragedy to open her eyes and suddenly she didn't like what she saw. Her family hadn't needed her all along. She had been the one using them to hide from herself.

Her face was expressive, changing from open bewilderment to misery and desolation. Resisting it violently, with enraged and defeated passion, she stared at Grandy.

He looked steadily back, his eyes filling with compassion.

She felt Sharon pushing a chair against the backs of her knees and sank gratefully on to it. The tears that had been dammed back for so long started welling up in her eyes and the more she tried to blink them away, the faster they came until she finally gave in. 'Oh, Grandy!' She buried her face in her hands and bent down to the bed.

His hand moved to rest heavily on her hair. 'Yes,' he murmured softly. 'I . . . knew . . . you would . . . see it . . . one . . . day.'

Sharon didn't really know what was going on but she sensed it was time to tactfully withdraw. Blowing a kiss to Grandy, she left the room.

Caroline felt forsaken and deserted and so terribly alone just as she had before, when she was left waiting at the church. Only this time she had nowhere to run. She was floundering. Instead of being the strong one everybody turned to for help, she was the weak clinging vine trying to hide from life behind her family. Even now, she was drawing comfort from Grandy instead of giving it to him.

David knew. He was a stranger but he had seen it at once. The thought was overwhelmingly humiliating.

After a while her breath became easier and the trembling in her body receded. 'I don't know what's the matter with me,' she hiccupped, wiping her eyes self-consciously. 'I used to be so strong. I thought I knew so much. I was so self-sufficient. Being jilted wasn't going to make me bitter.'

'We . . . all need . . . someone . . .' he struggled with the words. '. . . Even you.'

Her first impulse was to deny it. Her jaw clenched so tightly the bones in her face protested. 'Yes. Even me,' she said hoarsely, hating to admit it. For so long she had crushed the hurt, the pain and rage of being jilted, turning her back on it, refusing to face it and overcome it. She hadn't fooled anybody but herself by pretending she wasn't hurt. Now it stared her in the face and she didn't know how to cope. Instinct had her retreating further.

Smiling tearfully at Grandy to let him know she was all right, she gripped his hand hard and sat with him the rest of the afternoon but all the while, her mind was churning. Somehow, in that moment, she knew her whole life had changed.

That evening when Sharon and Caroline sat down to the meal Morwenna had kept warm for them, the boys rushed into the kitchen all talking at once, full of questions about Grandy. Caroline answered them in a subdued voice, smiling gently, passing on Grandy's witty messages to them. Her turbulent emotions were well hidden behind a cool bland mask. No one could tell by looking at her that her whole safe tidy world had been turned upside down.

A glass vase filled with wild flowers was centred on the big scrubbed table surrounded by a plate of home-made scones, slices of fruitcake and a big bowl of early strawberries.

Morwenna and David and her father were companionably sipping tea from her mother's best china cups and Caroline suddenly realised the house was becoming a home again. As hard as she'd tried this past year, she had never quite captured that elusive quality. Morwenna had done it at once, and instinctively.

Crushing down a rising sense of inferiority, she listened as Morwenna sent the boys back to their rooms to finish their homework and get ready for bed. It was nearing the end of the school year but she allowed no concessions to their routine.

David noticed that Caroline avoided looking directly at him all through her dinner and that her smile didn't really reach her eyes. He looked to Sharon as if she might tell him why but she was gazing at the flowers, lost in her own thoughts.

Each day that followed brought great strides to her father's as well as Grandy's progress. As one day slipped into another, her father became less vague. He still didn't say much but he began to take an interest in things around him and responded at meal times and often played a long silent game of chess with David in the evenings when David was there.

Every so often David and Sharon went out to a Saturday night dance or to a pub or simply to visit Sharon's friends on the neighbouring farms. To be polite, they invited Caroline along but she always made sure she had something pressing to do so as not to have to tag along. She went out of her way to be tactful and allow them their privacy.

John Polgearon wasn't as circumspect. He practically lived here these days. A tall thin man with dark hair and almost black eyes, he spent almost as much time with Sharon as David did. Caroline thought David must resent it but he never let on that it bothered him and she had to admire him for that.

Sharon was so in love. She no longer confided in Caroline now that Morwenna was so readily available but it was there in the way she moved, in her face, her every expression, her rapturous sighs. She stood gazing into space when it was her turn to do the dishes or scrub floors. Caroline watched her and shuddered without knowing why.

Then little by little she began to understand what was happening to her. Ugly, searing jealousy clawed at her whenever she happened to see Sharon and David together. When gentle looks passed between them, Caroline felt ridiculously affronted. A word, a gesture, even one of David's wide white smiles had the power to turn her into a bitter trembling mass of envy.

This is insanity, she told herself night after night. But her heart wouldn't listen. It went right on loving him. She *didn't* love him! She couldn't. She said it so many times it became a monotonous litany, as if saying it often enough would make it so. She didn't know anything about love. She wasn't capable of it any more—and certainly not with the man her sister loved.

When May turned into June, Grandy was well enough to come home. Caroline was the only one available to make the drive on the day he was discharged so she went alone to pick him up.

'Oh, stop fussing, Caroline!' he roared when she parked and tried to help him out of the car. His speech was back to normal. The only thing slowing him down now was a slight paralysis of his right leg and a partial blindness in one eye. He was thinner and whiter and looked almost gaunt after a month in hospital.

The doctor had given them a list of instructions when he discharged him and at the top of it was the warning that nothing was to upset him. Caroline wondered how long it would be before she broke that warning. Nothing was going right for her these days.

It had been a long ride home and dusk was falling. She was hot and tired. Grandy's foibles never bothered her before but lately she found herself close to tears over the slightest things. Her poise was slipping badly. Inside, she was falling apart and she couldn't do anything to stop it. Stepping back at once, unbearably hurt, she let David help Grandy from the car.

David's eyes glittered expressionlessly before he handed him his cane and gently led him up the walk where her father stood waiting for him.

Alexander Pentreath looked dark and virile in the fading light, the blue, open-necked shirt and jeans deceptively covering the thinness of his frame. 'Welcome home, Dad,' he said quietly, smiling at him.

No one had told Grandy. His eyes widened in stunned surprise before huge tears welled up in them. His mouth shook. 'Alec!'

Her father flew down the walk to him and embraced him, shaking so much he nearly fell. 'Oh, Dad!' he kept saying over and over. 'Oh, Dad!'

Caroline felt her own tears clogging her throat and turned away at once. Her father was well again. Everything would be the way it was before her wedding day had put a blight on all their lives.

Then all the others were there, gathering around them, laughing, crying, all talking at once. Caroline knew she wouldn't be missed for a while. Slipping away, she sought the solitude of the narrow stream running through the lower pasture where she could pull herself together without anyone but the placid brown cattle intruding.

Listening to the soothing murmur of water tripping over stones, she sighed heavily. Now that Grandy was home, she was sure it would just be a matter of time before Sharon and David announced their engagement. When that happened she didn't know if she'd be able to stand there and smile and offer them her good wishes. Her only alternative was to leave. Now. Before she made an even bigger fool of herself.

The rose and purple sunset was full of silence as twilight deepened. The wind began to rise and the sound of moving water became stronger. She clasped her hands behind her back and kicked angrily at the stones. She knew she had to go. But where? What could she do? She really wasn't qualified to do anything except take care of a family—and she hadn't even done that right.

Self-pity washed over her. She didn't even try to fight it this time. She hadn't taken care of her family. She had used them to hide from herself. That's all it was. Her fists bunched. Why wasn't strength and self-sufficiency there, just for the asking? She needed Philip Tregenna, trusted him, loved him, leaned on him, and look where it got her. She had turned into a bitter, twisted woman without even knowing it.

The sound of the sea beckoned and she

followed it without thinking. Even in this half light there was a soothing majesty to the great rugged boulders with the water swirling around their looming shapes. How could she even contemplate leaving this haven of peace? A sick feeling knotted her stomach. There was no place for her any more. She suddenly felt like an outsider, a pariah, she thought. She should have been called Ishmael.

The wind was wilder here on the high cliffs, stiffly blowing, carving her cotton dress harshly against her tall body. Her hair broke from its braid and whipped across her face.

'It's customary to leave a note,' a deep voice said from somewhere behind her.

Startled, her whole body jerked before she turned, her heart leaping to her throat.

David stood close to her, poised as if ready to lunge. Accusation was in his stance and that surprised her. His breath was coming quickly, his chest heaving under his frayed plaid shirt. He had been running, she realised. His sandy hair was wild about his head.

'A note . . .?' She frowned, not knowing what he was talking about. Then all at once her eyes widened and a spasm crossed her face when it hit her. 'I wasn't going to jump!' she cried angrily. 'I've got more brains than that!'

Some of his stiffness left him but still, he

came closer and gripped her arm tightly. 'How was I to know?'

'You'll just have to take my word for it,' she said coldly, trying to shrug off his hand. 'Will you let go of me, please?'

'I don't think I should. There's a little boy back there who'd never forgive me if anything happened to you.'

She jerked her arm out of his grasp and stepped away. A sound of disgust bubbled harshly in her throat. 'Tim doesn't need me any more. None of them do. They never did.'

A muscle flexed in his jaw but his voice remained quiet. 'I'm glad you realise they can get along without you, but I wasn't talking about any of your brothers. I meant my son.'

In spite of herself, her face softened when she thought of Steven but she stiffened it at once. He was just one more person she would use if given the chance. He deserved better than that. 'He doesn't even know me,' she said. 'Why should he care?'

David let that pass. 'He thinks he knows you,' he said softly. 'The important things, anyway.' Something like pain shimmered across his face. 'Just before you brought Grandy home tonight, we were talking. He asked me if his mother was as beautiful as you are.'

All her breath left her in a rush. The absurdity of such a comparison should have made her smile but for the first time in months she completely forgot her own problems and looked outside herself and an overwhelming sympathy quivered through her. It couldn't be easy for David to live with nothing but the memories of the gorgeous wife he had lost all too soon. 'Oh, David, I'm so sorry.' She knew no one could ever measure up to Judith. No woman in her right mind would even try. 'Doesn't he remember her at all?'

He shook his head. 'He was only three when she died. Before that, I had to leave him with sitters because she was in and out of hospital so much. He never really knew her.'

She drew a slow painful breath and thought she saw desolation in his face. 'Have you been able to talk to him about her? Show him photographs?'

'Oh, I've tried to tell him things to keep her alive for him, but last year we lost everything that belonged to her in a house fire.' He jammed his hands in his pockets and stood looking out to the empty expanse of moon silvered water. 'Nothing was left,' he murmured. 'Not even a photograph. She was completely gone, as if she had never been.'

Caroline swallowed past the huge dry lump in her throat. Her eyes squeezed shut on hot tears. It wasn't her place to cry but she couldn't help it. Judith was the epitome of refinement, of grace and gentleness and beauty. It wasn't right that she should be so completely lost to him. 'Oh, David,' she almost sobbed. 'I'm so sorry.'

She turned away so he wouldn't see her tears but he reached out and gently closed his arms around her, holding her tightly, resting his chin on the top of her head, softly stroking the long rigid line of her back.

'I didn't mean to make you feel bad,' he apologised.

She only shuddered helplessly and burrowed deeper into his chest and clung to him. If only there was something to say to ease his sorrow. But there was nothing, nothing at all.

They stood together for long minutes, not talking, not moving, each giving as well as taking comfort simply from the undemanding presence of the other.

Then it all began to change. It wasn't enough. In the dark sea-tossed silence, she swallowed nervously. His breathing was even and steady but hers seemed to stop altogether before it became strangling. She felt him tense and felt the quickening of his pulsebeat. What was it about him that made her long to be part of him? What kind of flame was this that tantalised and tormented no matter how hard she fought against it?

She knew she shouldn't be here in his arms with her shaking body fitted to the taut muscular length of his. But, oh, for the moment it was heaven! Her skin tingled in waves of pleasure. Her heart lurched and began to race, its rhythm thumping raggedly. Everything was forgotten: Judith, Sharon, her own painful memories of being jilted. They were simply a man and a woman together on a rocky Cornish cliff with the wind and the sea and the night all around them.

She lifted her darkening eyes to look him full in the face, wishing he would lower his head. She could almost taste the warmth of his lips moving back and forth on hers. The clean earthy scent of his body drifted on the wind, enveloping her, making her giddy.

If only she had the nerve to raise her arms to his neck and pull him closer, to press her body more firmly into the hard comfortable length of his, to revel in its languorous melting warmth. Her fingers itched to bury themselves in the tangled thickness of his hair, to stroke the planes of his face, to trace the fine lines crinkling at the corners of those bright blue eyes. She wanted to cup her palms to his throat and let the strong pulse beat against them, to slide and curl them mindlessly over his shoulders, to take his shirt from him so she could feel the pleasing texture of his skin.

A richness of feeling seemed to flow between them, gathering, swelling, until they both were breathing one breath. A fierce sweet passion enfolded her. The deep rawness of desire made her tremble. Her bones turned to water. Her whole body throbbed with the need to feel, to taste, to touch him.

But all she did was stand there, too shy to make the first move, too shy to do anything but look at him with her heart in her eyes.

I want to make love to you, Caroline.

She heard the words clearly enough but his lips hadn't moved. Had he said that? Really? Or had she imagined it? In her besotted state, was she putting words into his mouth?

Ice slithered down her spine. A roaring seemed to sound in her ears as suddenly everything came rushing back: who she was, who he was. Her stomach plunged in painful self-disgust. How could she feel this way? Think things like this? What madness possessed her? She, more than anybody, knew the kind of rejection she was inviting by letting him this close. Hadn't she learned her lesson in the most painful way possible? She was a jilted woman. There was some flaw in her. She wasn't good enough for any man.

She wouldn't trust. Ever again. No man would be given another chance to hurt her. And besides, there was Sharon. David had had the most beautiful wife in the world and now her beautiful sister was going to make him hers. How could she forget so completely?

Almost staggering backwards, she abruptly broke away from him, her eyes like huge greenish bruises in her white face.

'Caroline?' A flicker of hurt and confusion crossed his face before he let out a defeated breath and dropped his arms to his sides. He took a searching step towards her. 'What's wrong?'

She backed away further, her chin coming up defiantly as she tried to hide her embarrassment behind a proud look.

'I'll never understand you in a hundred years,' he muttered, his mouth twisting. 'I thought there was something between us . . . but I'm wrong, aren't I? You don't care for me at all.'

Nausea began to churn in her stomach. Had he forgotten Sharon too? Or did he get some kind of kick out of stringing them both along? Her mouth shook. 'I just remembered who you are!' she choked.

His head snapped back as if he couldn't believe she said that. He couldn't have looked more stunned if she'd struck him. Then his jaw hardened and he took a deep steadying breath before raggedly letting it out. 'I see,' he said quietly, but his voice had the choked softness of a dying man. He looked at her for another long minute almost in a daze. 'I didn't realise . . . what you've heard . . . I thought it didn't matter to you.'

It wasn't until he turned and walked away

that she realised he was trembling. What he said didn't make any sense. It was the gibberish of a stricken man. Somehow he had been wounded by her remark but she didn't know why. And then she told herself she was right to remind him who he was. He belonged to Sharon. She had to start now to make sure there'd be no awkward ghosts between them for him to remember once he became her brother-in-law.

She turned back to the cliff's edge and bit her lip, staring at the empty expanse of water until it became a blur of moon shimmered blackness. She had to leave soon. With each tossing crash of a wave, the refrain began again.

I don't love him. I don't love him.

CHAPTER SIX

THE next day Caroline wasted no time in starting to search for a job. As soon as old Mrs Trerhyn opened the post office, she went in to scan the jumbled notice board. Everything was tacked up here from 'Free cats to a good home' to a request from a dying boy in Scotland who wanted to get into the *Guinness Book of World Records* for having received more post cards than anyone else, but there was nothing that came anywhere near to being what she was looking for.

'Looking for something special, Caroline?' Mrs Trerhyn asked with a curious frown, watching as she methodically went through the notices.

'A job,' she said softly. 'You wouldn't know of anything, would you?'

'Not for you, my dear. Now if it was for that flighty sister of yours . . .'

Caroline looked up in surprise. She didn't realise Sharon had that reputation outside her family.

Mrs Trerhyn tottered to her place behind the counter and began sorting the day's post. 'I always told my Willy, God bless his soul,

Sharon should have been the one Philip Tregenna jilted, not you.'

A dull wave of colour began to run up Caroline's neck but Mrs Trerhyn went on blithely.

'Sharon would have shed her tears then gone on to someone else instead of letting it change her. But not you, dear. You're deep, that you are. Much too deep for the likes of Philip Tregenna.

'Now if you were to set your sights on David Tremain . . .' She rolled her rheumy blue eyes, '. . . there's the man for you. A real gentleman, he is. Why, I remember when he and that young whelp Jason Caine used to come in here. Two opposite ends of the social scale, they were: Jason with his millions and David without two coins to rub together. But you couldn't tell by looking at them which was which.' Her eyes softened with reminiscence. 'They were true gentlemen, both of them, and two closer friends you'd never find—until Judith Treloar came between them.'

She looked straight into Caroline's face and wagged a bony finger. 'Something funny there, mark my words. She was engaged to Jason, you know, but up and ran off to America with David. I never did believe all the gossip that followed them about David being the father of her child. He was too much of a gentleman to cause her that kind of hurt. Sir

James believed it, though. He disowned them and told David he'd never forgive him. He vowed he'd never see a penny of the money he thought he'd married.'

Caroline's heart gave a sudden painful thump. Even here she couldn't escape David. She would have liked to scream at Mrs Trerhyn to stop but she controlled herself. 'Please, Mrs Trerhyn,' she said softly, 'we really shouldn't be discussing David's personal affairs like this. We know nothing about his marriage to Judith.'

She looked slightly taken aback. 'What? Above a bit of a gossip, are you?'

'No. But I know first hand how much gossip can hurt.'

Mrs Trerhyn suddenly had the grace to look ashamed. 'I'd actually forgotten all the spiteful things said about you when Philip left . . . You're right, my dear. Forgive me.'

Caroline nodded unhappily and gave the notice board another cursory inspection.

All the next week she combed the newspapers for situations vacant but found nothing there either. Mrs Trerhyn offered to keep an eye and an ear open and Caroline knew she was burning with curiosity as to why she wanted a job but she couldn't tell her. She couldn't even discuss it with Morwenna for fear she would try to talk her out of it.

She managed to keep out of David's way

except at mealtimes when she had no choice. Not a word passed between them since that night on the cliffs. David was different now. Always a quiet man before, he became aloof and taciturn. His expression wasn't cold these days, but the craggy lines seemed to be etched deeper into his skin and his eyes weren't as bright and his mouth rarely curved into a smile even when he was alone with Sharon and his son.

David and Morwenna made no move to return to her house now that Grandy was better. Part of her wished they'd go but another more masochistic part of her was glad they stayed. She could watch him from a distance and dream her useless dreams and wish with utter futility that it all could be different.

Steven settled into the family as if he was born to it and try as she might, it was impossible for Caroline not to become more and more attached to him. He was always close to her side. Every once in a while she'd catch a flash of something in his face and a strange warm feeling would run through her. What it was or why it happened, she couldn't say. But there was something about him she couldn't quite put her finger on.

Maybe it was because David was his father, she told herself cynically, though a fat lot of good that did her. She should be discouraging this closeness not cultivating it.

It wouldn't be fair to leave Steven with yet another gaping hole in his life when she found employment and left him. And she would be leaving soon. There had to be a job for her somewhere.

Spring gently turned into summer but depression hung over her like a great black cloud growing darker with each passing day.

Her brothers were finished with school for the summer holidays and now the house was alive and pulsing with their sheer joy of living from morning until night. There were new lambs and calves. The trees were all in bloom and the earth was bursting with all the richness of its bounty but Caroline saw none of it. She went through the motions of living but she was just marking time and she knew it.

Steven was learning to ride a pony this bright sunny morning at the beginning of July and her brothers called her to join them. 'Come and watch, Caro,' they shouted, their voices ringing on the warm, flower-laden breeze.

She waved to them from her bedroom window. The flimsy excuses she gave to avoid such family gatherings as this were becoming transparent even to her so she didn't bother to think them up any more. She simply pretended she was too busy.

For some reason her heart squeezed painfully when she saw them all standing at the paddock watching Steven. Her father was next to Morwenna with his arm lightly resting across her shoulders. Sharon was sitting on the fence close to David but angled so that she was facing John Polgearon. When Caroline saw her bat her eyes at John and smile provocatively, rage rose in her throat. Sharon was too old for games like this. She didn't have to try to make David jealous. He wasn't the kind to respond to such tactics. He was already eating out of her hand. What more did she want? Blood? And it was wrong for her to lead John on. He'd become a good friend ever since Grandy's stroke and he deserved better treatment than that. Rob and Tim were perched on the fence, shouting encouragement and hooting while Mike led Steven round and round on the gentle pony. Grandy stood there, tall and still, his cane hooked over his arm, watching with a crooked smile.

Caroline's mouth curved gently. Grandy was so much better now. He rarely needed his cane any more but he still carried it with him whenever he was going to be outside for any length of time. She knew she would be out of place if she joined them. She didn't belong any more. She wondered if she ever did.

'Caroline? May I come in?' Morwenna's musical voice sounded behind her before she tapped lightly on the open bedroom door.

'Oh. Yes, of course.' She turned from the window and straightened the curtains self-consciously, chagrined to have been caught looking.

'We were wondering why you won't come to watch Steven,' she said softly without censure. 'He's very proud of his accomplishments.'

Caroline shrugged. 'I wanted to finish up a few things first.'

Morwenna looked at the piles of clothing that were sorted out and neatly folded on the bed. 'I'd like to think you were cleaning out your drawers but it looks more like you're getting ready to pack. Are you going somewhere?'

Stiffening, Caroline lifted her chin in a defensive gesture. 'That's right.'

'Oh, Caro.' A sad smile mingled with pity ran across her face. 'I used to be able to read you like a book but now you won't let me in. What's happened? Why are you thinking of leaving home?'

'No special reason. I've finally grown up, that's all.' She lifted her shoulders and shoved her hands in the back pockets of her jeans, giving her a breezy smile that didn't fool her for a minute. 'It's about time, don't you think?'

'Growing up doesn't mean you have to withdraw from your family. You never spend any time with them any more, except for

Steven. It's as though you're hiding away up here.' Her face creased into troubled lines. 'Do you want to talk about it?'

'There's nothing to talk about. Honestly.' Her smile faltered and became wooden. 'I've just been doing a lot of thinking lately and I've decided I need a change. If I can't find anything in the village, I may go to Penzance to find a job.'

Morwenna's eyes widened. 'But Caroline! You know you love the farm. You'd be lost doing anything else.'

'How do I know that? I've never tried anything else. Maybe I'll love it.'

Consternation was written all over her as she weakly subsided on to a straight-backed chair near the bed. 'Why, Caro? Why now?'

'It's time.' She pushed aside some of her clothes and sat on the edge of the bed and stared at her shoes. 'Remember after Philip jilted me? You said there's a time for everything? "To every thing there is a season . . ." ' she began to quote. 'Well, I've thought about it and,' she looked up and held her gaze steadily, 'you were right. When I loved Philip, it wasn't time for me to love. I never faced it before. All I did was hide behind my family for the past year and pretend it never happened. Now I've seen it for what it was. Philip didn't love me and I didn't really love him. I'm finally putting it behind me. Now it's time for me to go on.'

'I see.' Morwenna looked at her long and hard, knowing there was more to it but unable to see past the defensive barrier Caroline kept between them. 'Well then, if there's no changing your mind, will you do me one last favour before you go?'

She tilted her head. 'If I can.'

'Wait until after the wedding,' she said softly, her eyes full of tenderness, a broad smile tugging at her lips before helplessly spreading across her face.

But Caroline missed it. She sat staring straight ahead in stunned silence. Shock struck at her, and wild panic. She held her breath.

So, David finally did it! He'd asked Sharon to marry him. Her whole body stiffened as ice shuddered down her spine. She sat up straight and her mind began to spin and whirl and dip and plunge. Why hadn't she left sooner? This was just the thing she wanted to avoid. How could she offer David and Sharon congratulations and pretend to be happy for them?

A long shivering ran through her. Gripping her hands together, she stared blindly ahead, seeing them together in each other's arms, smiling at each other in all their wedding finery. Her breath became short and ragged and painful. Her heart roared. Her pale, bloodless face dampened with a sick flush.

'Caroline!' Morwenna's dreamy look was

completely erased. Real concern took its place. 'What is it?'

She struggled to find her voice and make it sound normal. How could she let herself behave like this in front of anyone? She knew it was coming. She should have been prepared. 'I'm sorry, Morwenna,' she choked, turning her face away before she betrayed too much. She had to get out of here but she couldn't move. The walls of her room, the sunlight, the breeze coming in the open window, the distant lowing of cattle and the murmur of the sea merged together in a great blinding swirl before her.

Morwenna took her cold clammy hands and forcibly squeezed them, chafing the skin almost frantically. 'I never expected this kind of reaction from you. I thought you'd be happy for me. You know I've loved your father for a long time.'

The blinding red mist began to clear from her eyes. She saw Morwenna standing in front of her but it was as if from a great distance and through a darkened tunnel. 'You love my father?' she repeated stupidly. Her lips moved stiffly. It made no sense to her.

'He asked me to marry him last night,' she said. 'We didn't mention it to the others yet. I wanted you to be the first to know.'

Caroline's shoulders sagged. She swallowed

noisily and felt as if something was running out of her. The tight constriction around her heart lessened and she looked at Morwenna as if she'd never seen her before. Her eyes were almost pleading. 'My *father* asked *you* to marry him?' she whispered. '*That's* the wedding you're talking about?'

'Why, yes. Whose did you think I meant?'

Caroline's face flushed deeply. The breath she had been holding suddenly left her in a noisy rush. Shudders ran over her skin and a brilliant relieved smile broke like sunshine across her face. 'Oh, Morwenna!' She shot to her feet and hugged her tightly, helplessly, almost giddy with relief. David wasn't marrying Sharon yet. There was still time for her to get away. 'Oh, I'm so happy for you. And even happier for Daddy. You'll be so good for him.'

Morwenna smiled back through a frown. 'Are you sure?'

'Oh, yes!' she laughed. 'I knew there was something between you. I just didn't realise—oh, I'm so glad!'

'Thank you, Caro,' she said softly, still not convinced that she was all right. 'I know I'm not the biggest prize in the world but I hope to make your father happy.'

'Of course you will. When do you plan to tell the others?'

She blushed delicately. 'Well, since they're all together right now . . . How about it? Will you come with me? Lend us your moral support?'

Caroline couldn't refuse. 'Of course.' She smiled widely, linking her arm through hers.

'And will you be my bridesmaid?'

'If you want me.'

'You're my best friend—though now I'll be your wicked stepmother. I wouldn't dream of having anyone else.'

Caroline laughed delightedly, a full rich sound that rang around the room. 'Wicked stepmother. I like that.'

When they reached the paddock, Steven was sitting awkwardly in his saddle but his smile stretched from ear to ear.

'Look, Caro! I'm riding!' he shouted, gripping the saddle horn with both hands.

'That's wonderful, darling.' She grinned at him. Going up to her father, she slid her arm around his waist. 'And it's wonderful about you as well, Dad.'

He looked sheepishly at her before wrapping an arm about her and gathering Morwenna to his other side. 'You don't think I'm an old fool?'

'You'd only be a fool if you let her get away from you.'

'Ah-h-h.' There was a wealth of satisfaction in the word as he gently kissed the top of Caroline's head. 'Thank you, my dear. You don't think the others will see it as a betrayal of your mother?'

'Not at all,' she said seriously, trying to erase the slight frown on his brow. 'They love you too much to think that. It's time for you to be happy again—and Morwenna's so right for you, for all of us.'

He nodded and squeezed her gently before turning to smile at Morwenna. Clearing his throat, he looked to the rest of his family. 'There's something I'd like you all to know,' he said in a curiously nervous voice that caught their attention immediately. 'Last night I asked Morwenna to marry me.'

For a moment there was total silence then suddenly they all began crowding around and talking at once.

'Great!' Tim shouted, hopping up and down. His little face was beaming.

'Super!' Rob bellowed. He looked at Morwenna and grinned. 'I knew Daddy never had a chance once you decided he needed you.'

'Oh, how wonderful!' Sharon clapped her hands and swung on the fence, letting a fatuously grinning John lift her down.

A warm knowing smile crossed David's face when he looked at them but he didn't say anything.

Grandy scowled because it was expected of him but he couldn't quite contain a broad grin. 'And what did Morwenna say when you asked her?' he asked, as if there was any doubt.

Alec laughed self-consciously. 'She said she's already seen me at my worst.' His face softened when he looked down into her lambent eyes. 'She's willing to take a chance on me.'

'Chance,' Grandy snorted. 'That has nothing to do with it. I saw her looking at your tea leaves last night. She's the most dangerous kind of woman there is. She'll always know what you're thinking. I told you to drink coffee.' His smile took the sting out of his words and Morwenna laughed delightedly when he stepped forward to kiss her.

Michael, who was leading Steven's pony, let out a loud whoop of delight without thinking. It startled both Steven and the horse and he reared back, tumbling Steven to the ground.

Before anyone else could move, Caroline vaulted over the fence and was the first to reach him. 'Are you all right?'

His little arms circled her neck, nearly choking her, and he pressed his face into her shirt front dampening it with his tears.

'It's all right to be afraid,' she soothed, 'but are you hurt?'

He shook his head but wouldn't release his choking hold.

After a minute his trembling body was prised loose and he was held high in his father's arms. 'You'll be all right, Steve. It wasn't a bad fall. You know what you have to do, don't you?' David said softly.

Steven leaned back looking straight into his eyes without wavering then he looked to Caroline. Biting his lips, he buried his face into David's neck, shuddering helplessly. 'I can't.'

'Steven,' he murmured gently, stroking his back, 'If you don't get right back on, you'll probably never ride a horse again. You'll be too afraid. You don't want that, do you?'

'That's right,' Mike added, coming up behind them with the pony. 'It was my fault the horse threw you. I startled him and he reared back. You didn't fall off because you did something wrong. How about it? Won't you try again? You were having so much fun.'

Steven took a deep shuddering breath before sliding out of David's arms. The saddle looked an awfully long way up but, squeezing his eyes shut, he reached for it and awkwardly lifted his leg and swung himself up.

'Like a pro,' Mike soothed.

For a minute he nearly lost his seat as the pony sensed his fear and began to shuffle nervously.

Caroline instinctively started forward but David's hands shot out, forcibly holding her back.

'No. Don't touch him. Let him do it.'

It was the right thing to say and Caroline knew it but her oversensitive emotions where David was concerned had her twisting it out of proportion. Of course, she was babying Steven and he couldn't have that, could he? She turned, her eyes locking with his for a screaming instant before she finally looked again at Steven. Trying to shrug her arm out of David's grasp, he merely tightened his grip and pulled her out of the way, moulding her back against his long frame.

'Watch,' he said from somewhere behind her ear.

Steven's face was white with anxiety as he tried to regain his balance. 'I'm not scared,' he said to nobody in particular.

In a bold gesture, David said quite softly: 'Hand him the reins, Mike. Steven, see if you can guide the pony to us.'

Us. The word shivered through Caroline. There was no us even though she and David were standing so close together she could feel every hard warm muscle in his body pressed against her back. They might have been the only two people there, she thought with a quivering ache. Everything was so intensely quiet and still.

David's voice was firm with all the confidence in the world in his son's ability to handle himself, but his grip on Caroline's arms was bone crushing.

She could feel the fine trembling in him

and hear the irregular thudding of his heartbeat. Without thinking, her arms crossed in front of her and her hands covered his on her shoulders, squeezing hard to let him know she felt the same. This might have been their son they were watching with such exclusive concentration. For a moment the thought ran through her and made her weak.

Almost in slow motion, Steven brought the pony forward without any mishap. David shuddered against Caroline for one more long second then stepped away and lifted him out of the saddle.

'You did it!' he congratulated him, swinging him high in his arms.

'Well, young man, you stole my thunder,' Alec said with a laugh. 'But you've all the makings of a good rider. Anyone can see that.'

The excited babble of laughter and congratulations and best wishes once again washed over them as they all started for the house. Only Caroline was left standing alone in the paddock, her shaking hands absently stroking the pony's nose when he nuzzled her pocket for an apple.

A rush of loneliness shivered through her and an overwhelming sense of loss now that David had gone. Get used to it, she told herself. This is the way it will be when you finally leave. Her throat constricted when her eyes involuntarily swept over the house and yard and barn. But all she really saw was David. This was her home. Everything she ever wanted was here. David was here. How could she think of leaving? Yet how could she stay? With Morwenna taking her mother's place, nothing would be the same. And it would change even more when David and Sharon . . .

She swallowed convulsively and felt a harsh sob rising uncontrollably in her throat. Why couldn't she think of anything else? Why did everything always have to come back to David? God, she was beginning to hate the sound of his name.

CHAPTER SEVEN

As much as she hated to admit it, Caroline dreaded the approaching wedding. Not because she wasn't happy for her father and Morwenna, but because she couldn't help comparing it to her own ill-fated one. It was going to be held in the same church, the ceremony performed by the same vicar, the reception in the same parish hall.

She knew her family couldn't help making comparisons either, although they were careful not to mention it in her hearing. The sudden silences when she walked into a room, the pitying looks, the careful conversations made her want to scream. Finally she began taking long solitary walks along the cliffs to ease the situation. If nothing else, it would remove her dampening presence for a little while.

She couldn't come right out and say to them; 'Look, it doesn't really hurt any more. Go ahead and make your plans. Be happy. Talk about it openly. Don't let me stop you.' No, she couldn't say that. For one thing, her vehemence would shock them. For another, it wouldn't be true. Talk of weddings did make her nervous. It made her sense of humiliation immediate instead of letting it stay in the past. As hard as she tried, there was no way to forget that she had been left waiting at the church with her hopelessly romantic dreams of 'happily ever afters' crumbling in ruins around her. Philip was dead and there was no way to find out why he left her without a word of explanation. The only one who could tell her was her father and it had been so traumatic for him she couldn't risk bringing it up again. She told herself it was for the best that she didn't know. She'd just think of it as one of life's mysteries.

So she took to walking. Sometimes Steven tagged along, sometimes Tim and the dog. Most often she was alone.

There was something so soothing about nature, she thought, shoving her hands deep in the pockets of her jeans. The water swirled about the huge granite boulders at the bottom of the cliffs this sunny afternoon toward the end of July. The sky was a brilliant blue with small tufts of white clouds looking oddly fragile in the endless enormity of space before her. The grass was rough beneath her feet and for a distance, where the path ran close to a little-used road, colourful wild flowers grew with abandon, tumbling down the cliff to the bay. All alone, Caroline followed them and took off her shoes and wiggled her toes at the edge of the rippling water. The wind was whipping the surface into a splashing white foam and sunlight scattered itself across the waves like liquid diamonds. Sea gulls screamed overhead, raucously wheeling and soaring against the sky. The tang of the salt-laden air filled her senses with pleasure.

How much longer would she be free to indulge herself like this, she wondered. The wedding was tomorrow and she made up her mind to leave after that. But where would she go? She was unemployable, fit for nothing. If only people still sought governesses, she thought, and then she had to laugh at herself. That was no help. The Cornish School Board would have something to say about her lack of qualifications.

She aimlessly kicked at the spray of an oncoming wave. If only she was a heroine in a novel. Why couldn't she be a Jane Eyre on her way to a happy ending at Thornfield Hall? Why couldn't David be an Edward Rochester? Her mouth twisted. Why couldn't it be that simple . . .?

She didn't know what made her sense she wasn't alone any more but turning around and looking up, she saw David standing at the edge of the cliff watching her. Surprise rippled through her, as if thinking about him could suddenly make him appear, and then, inexplicably, she became angry.

He easily loped down the boulder-strewn

cliff and drew near, his handsome face inscrutable. 'Hello, Caroline,' he said quietly. The clear blue of his eyes matched the bright summer sky behind him.

'Have you been following me?' she accused.

'Now why would I do that?' His soft tone of voice didn't change nor did the small smile hovering at the sides of his mouth.

Her anger swiftly turned to embarrassment. 'I——' She couldn't find an answer and to her chagrin, mortified colour began to run up her neck. She stood there at a loss, hungrily drinking in the exquisite shape of his tall body in jeans and a blue homespun shirt. A lock of hair had fallen across his forehead and she had the absurd urge to reach out and smooth it back and feel the warmth of his skin and the silky softness of his hair against her fingertips. She was assailed by a familiar bursting in her heart, a yearning she had to learn to control. 'I'm sorry. I don't know why I thought that.'

'It's an honest enough mistake.' He bent down and picked up several small pebbles near her feet. 'Do you mind if I join you?'

He was looking at her bare feet and her toes involuntarily curled and dug into the gravelly silt. She felt gauche all of a sudden, as if she'd been caught doing something wrong. 'No, of course not.' The nonchalance she tried to project became more of a breathless stammer. She twisted her hands behind her back to keep them from blindly reaching out to him of their own volition.

He laughed softly and took off his boots. 'Nothing like paddling on a beautiful summer day, is there?'

It was a question but he didn't expect an answer. He was looking out to the horizon, skipping stones across the water with the breeze full in his face, the collar of his shirt flapping against his back. By the looks of him, pleasant thoughts were occupying his mind and Caroline stood silently beside him, trying to stop the rapid drumming of her heart that assaulted her every time he was near.

Why did he have to be so handsome? It really wasn't fair to all the other men in the world. She tried to picture Philip, to compare them, but his face remained a hazy blur. All she could see was David's profile, the softly blowing sandy hair, the fine crinkling lines at the corner of his eye, the fascinating bump on the bridge of his nose, the compelling line of sensuality sculpting his lips.

He slowly turned to her and smiled, a gentle smile as if he knew she'd been studying him and he didn't want to startle her.

Her colour mounted and she wanted to say something to cover her embarrassment but all of a sudden her mind went completely blank. All she could do was stand there like an idiot looking at him. Something began to splinter inside her when she thought that all too soon she'd be leaving him. How could she live without him? How could she even think of going away and never seeing him again?

'Morwenna tells me you're leaving,' he said in a husky voice.

She swallowed hard and dropped her eyes almost guiltily. He knew how she felt, that she didn't really want to go. How could he walk around in her mind like that? It wasn't fair. She never knew what he was thinking. 'That's right,' she breathed. 'I have to go.'

'Why?'

'What do you mean, "why"?' She shrugged her shoulders and tried to sound flippant but it was to stall for time. She couldn't tell him it would break her heart to stay and see him married to Sharon. And if she tried to make up some excuse, he'd see through it in a minute.

'I never thought you'd run, Caroline,' he said roughly. 'I always thought behind that stubborn streak you had a quiet steady strength but I'm wrong, aren't I?' His voice shook and the sound made her look up, startled. He went on raggedly: 'You're a fool, do you know that? A fool!'

She knew that. He didn't have to tell her. Pain shimmered in her eyes and she started to turn away but his fingers gripped her chin, pulling her face up to look at him.

'All you do is mope around feeling sorry for yourself. Do you think you're the only woman who was ever jilted?'

She didn't want to hear any platitudes about putting the past behind her. 'Leave me alone!'

His hands moved to grasp her upper arms and pull her close to his tall lean length. 'No! Somebody's got to make you see you're not really a martyr. Philip didn't love you and you know it. He was a weakling. All he thought about was himself. He doesn't deserve to have you pining away for him. You never had the chance to know what love really was.'

'You don't know——' the tears gathering in her throat choked her, cutting off what she wanted to say, then they welled up to her eyes before spilling over.

'Oh, Caroline.' His hands tightened and a white ring of pain twisted his lips. 'I do know. If he really loved you, he would have been a haven of security for you. He wouldn't have left you alone and open and vulnerable to all the calumnies of this world. He would have told you why he couldn't marry you then he would have stayed and made sure you were protected from the gossip that was bound to follow. He would have waited before leaving for America.'

Something in his voice reached her and made her stiffen abruptly and stare up at him in confusion. Her eyes suddenly widened and were distended and glazed with tears. 'You know, don't you?' she whispered. 'You know why he left me. I know you do!'

He helplessly pulled her against him and pressed her face into his shoulder, shuddering, his warm heavy hands gently stroking her hair. 'Oh, Caro, Caro. I don't know why he left you. I could only guess and that wouldn't be fair to him or to you. Just put it behind you. Remember only that he didn't love you.'

Her rigid body was clenched to his and she was so tempted to sob out her anguish and frustration but she couldn't take advantage of him like that. Somehow she had to restrain the impulse. It was unworthy of her. A long minute later she pulled herself together again. Dragging a hand across her face, she breathed deeply, thankful that David's presence was so undemanding. He just stood there with her draped all over him, not saying anything. A true gentleman, she thought. He was letting her search for her scattering dignity and find it without making her feel stupid. She only hoped Judith had appreciated what a gem of a husband . . .

The thought screeched to a halt and she stopped dead, practically goggling into David's face with wide stretched eyes. A fine quivering ran through her and she felt hot and cold at the same time. Her heart began to pound with fast ragged thumps. Her arms involuntarily went up around his back again. 'That's what you did for Judith, isn't it? *That's* why you can say Philip didn't love me with such conviction. You weren't like him. You didn't leave Judith. You were her security. By taking her to America you were trying to protect her from wagging tongues.'

He closed his eyes on a spasm of remembered pain and dropped his arms and took a step backward. But she had her arms clasped around his back and stayed with him.

'Oh, David, Mrs Trerhyn from the post office told me there was all kinds of gossip when you married Judith so quickly—even your father-in-law, Sir James——' She broke off, nearly choking. 'But she never believed it for a minute. She said she knew you were too much of a gentleman to ever compromise Judith.'

His head went back and he smiled silently at the sky. 'So, I wasn't a beast in everyone's eyes after all. Well, well, well. Someone actually gave me the benefit of the doubt. After all this time, it's nice to know.'

Caroline stared at him and tried to see into his eyes but he wouldn't look at her. Putting her hands to either side of his face, she pulled his head down to her. 'Who is Steven?' she said fiercely.

He stiffened. A cold mask began to move over his features. His mouth hardened and his jaw jutted forward. 'He's my son.'

'Because you gave him your name not because you gave him life.'

'Leave it, Caroline.'

'No. I don't want to leave it. Who is he? You married Judith to protect her and her child, not because you were her baby's father.'

He reached up and pried her hands loose, keeping them crushed in his, his mouth set in implacable lines. 'Forget it.'

'How can I forget something like that?'

'It's none of your business, that's how!'

Her head jerked back as if he'd struck her and her breath bubbled harshly in her throat. 'Oh!' she said in a stunned voice. 'What's the matter with me? Of course, I had no right to even ask you such a thing!'

Shame and embarrassment and self-recrimination swirled through her mind and she started to turn away but he stopped her, tightening his hands and sighing in apology. 'No, don't say that. You, of all people, have a right to ask. I know it's not just idle curiosity with you. I think you love Steven almost as much as I do. I've just . . .' he breathed deeply, '. . . never been able to talk to anyone about it before.' He squeezed her hands once more, staring into her face for a long minute before letting her go and turning back to face the constantly churning water.

Her heart went out to him. If only there was something she could say. But all she could do was stand there helplessly, knowing she really had no right to say anything. She was wrong to go stirring up these painful memories for him. 'I'm so sorry,' she whispered.

He didn't hear her. His sight was turned inside himself and unbearable hurt stood out in the slumping line of his wide shoulders. 'It was a long time ago,' he said quietly, murmuring almost to himself. 'Judith came to me and asked for help and I couldn't let her down. She was engaged to my best friend, Jason Caine, at the time. But she said if she went to him or to her father, they would never understand. They were too crazy about her. They had put her on a pedestal and it would kill them to find that she was human after all.' He slid his hands through his hair and bunched them at the back of his neck. 'She was pregnant,' he said in a toneless voice, 'and the man wouldn't marry her. So I did. I tried to let her keep her respectability and tried to let Jason and Sir James keep their illusions.'

'Oh, David!' Shattered by such selfless generosity, she could feel the tears clogging her throat and blinked rapidly to keep them from springing to her eyes.

'Don't feel sorry for me,' he said. The wind loosened her braid and blew her long hair into his face. He curled his fingers around it, wiping it out of his eyes, letting the silky strands cling to them. 'Jason didn't speak to me for a long time after that but we finally sorted it out and now we're friends again. I was even best man at his wedding earlier this year. Some day the time will be right to talk to Sir James. Until then . . .' He shrugged and let the thought hover. 'Judith's dead now but I've never regretted helping her. If I had to do it all over again, I'd do the same thing. And look what she gave me: her son to call my own. What more could a man ask for?'

The noble words were full of humble simplicity and it made her want to sob. No other man would see only the good and be content with that. His sensitivity touched her and made her love him even more. A terrible yearning shivered through her until it actually became a physical ache.

'I keep making you feel bad,' he said gently, turning and looking at her before hooking an arm around her shoulders and gathering her close, 'but I don't mean to. I just want you to know you're not alone. You're not the only one trying to live down gossip. For whatever it's worth, I'll be there tomorrow. It's bound to be difficult for you, the same church and vicar and all, but I'll be there. If you'll let me, I'll be there for all your tomorrows.'

'Oh, David.' Was she really hearing this? Or was it a dream, something she conjured up in the lonely recesses of her heart. '*David*.' His name was full of passionate despair. She had no right to even think of taking what he offered. He belonged to her sister.

He kissed her gently, wanting to soothe her, his lips brushing her forehead before touching the corner of her eye and sliding along her cheek until he found the trembling softness of her mouth.

An involuntary response swept through her at his indulgent touch. She was caught and trapped in the bright tantalising flame of desperation and desire. Her heart fluttered and started banging against her ribs and she had trouble breathing. She wanted to give and wanted to take, wanted him to know all the things she had no right to say. Instinctively her hands resting on his arms slid up past his neck to curl and tighten in the shining thickness of his bright hair. Sanity fled. Here in his arms there were no yesterdays, no tomorrows, only today, now, this moment. Only the two of them.

Let me love you, Caroline.

She heard him, though his lips hadn't moved, and she looked at him with a wild blinding surge of love and longing. *Yes, yes, yes*! her heart answered.

Somehow her hands found their way inside his shirt, unashamedly trembling over the wide clenching muscles of his chest. She had never touched a man like this before. Her senses whirled and the sweet ache of desire swept through her, making her boneless and pliant in his arms. The warmth of his skin seared through her and she felt his mouth on hers once more, his kiss hardening with possession.

His own hands weren't idle. The tips of his fingers slid from her jaw to the curve of her neck, softly stroking its long line, drawing her closer, absorbing her quivers. The hard contours of his body moved against hers in an intimate caress. Deftly opening the buttons on her blouse, he found her breast and let its warm swelling softness spill into his quivering hand. It was a new sensation of intimacy for her and she moved shyly against him, trusting him implicitly. He wouldn't hurt her, not this gentle, humble, masterful man. Her heart stopped at the unspoken passion and promise of his hand on her breast. A heady sensuality flooded through her and had her legs buckling.

David circled his other arm around her back, his fingers tangling in her long brown hair, 'My little love,' he murmured against her lips.

Little? she thought dazedly. Love? No one ever called her little and no one ever really loved her before. He made her feel fragile and delicate. *Oh, David, I do love you.* Her heart spoke to his.

Very slowly he pulled a little away from her and looked deeply into her eyes. His face was serious then all at once the craggy lines softened and he smiled at the delicate flush on her cheekbones and the luminous glow in her eyes. 'You're something very special to me, Caro. You won't be leaving after your father and Morwenna are married?'

It was a question but also an unspoken command and she tingled with pleasure. Her heart began to sing. She wouldn't be leaving after all. He loved her as she loved him. 'I—I'll have to talk with Sharon,' she stammered, suddenly becoming conscious of their dishevelment. Shyly pulling away from him, she turned and fumbled with her blouse, wondering why she was all thumbs. Somehow she'd have to make Sharon understand that it just happened. It wasn't anything planned but she couldn't deny she belonged to David. Sharon might be hurt for a while but Caroline didn't think her emotions were all that deeply involved, especially the way she was always flirting with John Polgearon in front of David.

David laughed softly. 'Sharon will be glad you're staying. With your father and Morwenna going to Spain on their honeymoon, she'd never cope with the family by herself.' His smile was wry as he buttoned his shirt and smoothed back his hair. 'Not the way she's mooning about the house these days.'

Caroline tried to keep her composed façade. 'Well, she thinks she's very much in love.'

'With Sharon, you never know. She falls in and out of love so much.' He slipped a brotherly arm across her shoulders and picked up her shoes and his boots. Pulling her close to him, he started back along the rocky path. 'I've heard weddings have a habit of producing a startling chain reaction of other weddings, so maybe we'll find out if it's real this time.'

She frowned, a niggling unrest creeping into her mind at the way he said that, but she pushed it away at once not wanting to ask him what he meant, preferring to be dazzled instead by the sheer glory of being in love with him. David was hers now, at least he would be once she talked to Sharon then freely acknowledged it. Somehow she'd make Sharon see that she and David were meant for each other.

But in the last minute flurry of wedding preparations, Caroline had to wait to talk to her sister.

Morwenna made a beautiful bride. Her dress, a short-sleeved, knee-length vision of ivory chiffon, was softly gathered at the waist and swirling about her legs. She wore flowers in her hair and carried a tiny bouquet of warm wet violets.

Standing at the back of the church waiting for the guests to get situated in their pews, Caroline waited for the pain and humiliation to engulf her at the remembrance of how she must have looked to her family and friends last year when she stood in this very spot waiting for her errant groom. Always before she had only to think of it for the shame to become immediate but today nothing happened. It was as if Philip had jilted some other girl. She stood back, remembering, but somehow it couldn't touch her.

She was confused, standing there watching Mrs Trerhyn adjust her hat and twitch her dress as she tottered to her pew. It seemed incredible that she had let Philip twist her whole life. She knew if he hadn't died, if he could somehow come back, he'd be the last person she'd fall in love with now. She was a different person and that made her whole conception of love different as well.

Then, love was all moonlight and roses, soul stirring kisses and blind devotion, a sense of wonder and enchantment colouring all her world. Now, she realised love had many other facets and not all of them were wonderful.

If what she felt for Philip had been real, it would have endured. There would have been no sobering disillusionment when she found Philip so weak a man that he couldn't tell her face to face why he wouldn't marry her. If it had been love, he would have come to her and she would have tried to understand and if he needed forgiving, she would have been able to forgive him anything. But it hadn't been love. He didn't come to her. She didn't understand and she couldn't forgive him, even now. What they shared hadn't lasted or made her safe or protected her against the hurt life had to offer. Real love would have done that, she knew with certainty.

Philip's desertion had left her alone and vulnerable but now it was no longer terrifying. She was free of the past. Really free!

She gave Morwenna's dress a last-minute adjustment and revelled in the incredulous euphoria of the moment. She was free!

Grandy came just then and looked appraisingly at them. 'Very lovely,' he said gruffly, fingering the frail violets in Morwenna's bouquet. 'Alec is a lucky man.'

Morwenna blushed and gave him a dazzling smile, her face soft and radiant. 'I'm the lucky one.'

He turned his gaze to Caroline in a swirling knee-length dress of delicate rose jersey. 'Your father's been pacing the floor all morning—as if he was afraid his bride wouldn't show up.'

Morwenna stiffened but Caroline merely smiled at him.

'He shouldn't have worried. Morwenna loves him. She wouldn't do that to him.'

'That was uncalled for,' Morwenna said, her eyes flashing at Grandy.

'Oh?' He wasn't the least bit contrite. 'It's what everyone's thinking. I'm the only one with nerve enough to bring it out in the open, that's all.'

Morwenna opened her mouth to answer him back but Caroline put a restraining hand on her arm. 'Don't upset yourself, Morwenna. This is your day and nothing's going to mar it.' She turned to her grandfather and gave him a full blown smile that wasn't at all forced. 'You're right. It probably is on everyone's mind. I did think about Philip this morning. And coming here, I couldn't help remembering how he jilted me. But you know what?' Her laugh was soft and free. 'It doesn't hurt any more. It's gone. All of it. All the hurt and humiliation. He didn't love me or he wouldn't have done it. It's taken me a long time to admit it but I never really loved him either.'

The old organ wheezed to life just then and Caroline gave Morwenna's arm a squeeze and Grandy a smile and floated down the aisle to meet David, her father's best man.

Alec stood beside Morwenna at the altar,

tall and still in a stark black suit, his face radiant, his dark eyes brimming with love.

Caroline smiled indulgently at them and then was caught by David's sudden jerky movements when he hastily searched in all his coat pockets for the rings and couldn't find them.

'They're on your finger, Daddy!' Steven hissed from the front pew, shattering the solemnity of the moment.

David reddened and Morwenna and Alec laughed and Caroline forgot to be nervous throughout the rest of the ceremony.

The entire day was a success as far as she was concerned. Every time she thought of Philip, she would look at David and he would smile back, making her heart soar. Grandy enjoyed himself at the reception as well. Smiling benignly, he watched his family greet their guests with pride and dignity. He was sure some of the villagers were curious, having heard the gossip about the effect Caroline's jilting had on her father. But seeing her sitting with her brothers or talking quietly with small groups of men and women or making sure Tim and Steven didn't become bored and start getting into mischief, they knew their information had been wrong.

Alec looked perfectly normal, a besotted bridegroom, and Caroline glowed with an inner radiance that had them wondering who the lucky man was who put it there. Sharon flirted outrageously with John, and Rob and Mike tried to dodge several of the more persistent girls who made it plain they thought the Pentreath boys were inordinately handsome.

It took several days to return to normal but Alec and Morwenna left for their honeymoon and things eventually settled down and once again became routine.

Caroline came downstairs on a bright morning three days after the wedding having made up her mind this was the day to talk to Sharon. She had scrubbed the bathroom floor and was walking into the kitchen with the bucket and scrubbing brush. 'I thought I heard John's car on the drive,' she said.

Sharon looked up from where she was standing by the sink folded tightly in David's arms, her face glowing, a bright diamond ring sparkling on her finger. 'Oh, look, Caro. Isn't it beautiful? I'm finally going to be married!'

Caroline could only stand there, transfixed, looking at them, not believing what she was seeing. David's tall broad body was curved around Sharon. His hands were on her back and shoulder and his mouth was smeared by a bright red imprint of Sharon's lipstick. Wave after wave of rioting emotions struck at her. She couldn't have been more stunned if she had suddenly been poleaxed. A horrible twisting pain splintered in her heart and she trembled. All her breath left her. Her face paled and became rigid. The room swayed and rocked and tilted. Everything was falling down around her head with the force of an ocean behind it.

She saw David untangle himself from Sharon, taking a step toward her. 'Caroline!' she heard as if from a great distance.

Automatically jerking back, she swallowed convulsively and dredged up an instinctive dignity from somewhere deep inside. Her eyes were distended and she never took them off him. In some strange way she felt almost hypnotised. No matter how hard she tried, she couldn't drag her eyes away from him. Oh, David. *David*. He'd never know what it cost her to stand and face them with such resolute calmness when everything inside her was dissolving and bleeding out of her. How could he do this to her? He knew how much she loved him.

Forcing the words out in a wooden voice, she almost managed to smile at him. 'Congratulations. I wish you every happiness.'

She turned in a stupefied daze, setting down the bucket with a noisy splash and practically plunged back up the stairs to her room and for the first time in years, turned the lock. There was a noisy clamouring in her brain, a roaring in her ears, a red mist behind her eyes. This time she thought she would surely die.

CHAPTER EIGHT

How could he? *How could he?* After what they shared. It took a while but the realisation slowly began to dawn on her and Caroline saw just how much she had taken for granted. David never actually said he loved her. Her heart listened but heard only what it wanted to hear. Never mind the kisses they shared, the intimate embraces, the ardent smiles. They were simply mad impulses on his part, brotherly gestures that had got out of hand, moments out of time. They didn't mean a thing. Her overactive imagination had given them a significance all out of proportion to what they really were. What a fool, what a stupid, blind fool she was!

When David asked her to stay, she thought it was because he wanted her for himself. Now she realised it was because he needed her to take care of her family, leaving him free to pursue Sharon.

Deep racking shudders ran over her body as she lay face down in a broken heap on her bed, clenching the spread with stricken fists. Humiliation swamped her. How had she let this happen? She, who always wanted to be self-sufficient, who knew that love was not to be trusted, who knew if one said hello the time would have to come to say goodbye, had rushed headlong into that trap again. Oh, how brilliant! Why didn't she just hang a sign around her neck that said, 'Hurt this girl. She's stupid enough to fall for a man.'

It wasn't as if she was some unsuspecting, naïve innocent who didn't know the first thing about it. First Philip, now David. Tears welled up in her eyes. It was bound to happen sooner or later. It always did. She had ignored her instincts and let herself trust a man so there was no excuse this time. She had no one but herself to blame.

In spite of herself, she kept reliving those moments with him over and over, torturing herself with the thought that never again would he hold her in his strong yet gentle arms, never again would he kiss or caress her, never again arouse in her that trembling awareness and passion that had been so new and so irresistibly fascinating.

Giving in to self-pity and rage and disgust, she silently sobbed out all her pain. When she finally fell into a fitful doze, it was only to dream distressfully of Sharon and David in each other's arms.

She woke later in the afternoon and knew there was no hope for anything any more. Despair haunted her. She was alone, totally, irrevocably alone. Pain and desolation wrung her heart as she automatically bathed her face and braided her hair and mechanically changed her creased blouse. Like a puppet with no will of her own, her feet carried her down the stairs and out of the house toward the cliffs.

A gentle wind was blowing through the bracken and the sun was pressing down on her shoulders in a shimmering haze of warmth. Always before, she could find a healing peace in the sound of the waves hurling themselves against the rocks below and in the way the sun-sprinkled water rushed forward and back with monotonous regularity. Her instincts had her looking for surcease but it was not to be found here today. She didn't see the rugged beauty of the sunwarmed cliffs all about her. Her eyes were blind to the bobbing wildflowers tumbling in the grass. She didn't hear the raucous screech of the gulls overhead. She didn't notice the play of sunlight and shadow as the fleecy clouds drifted across the afternoon sky. All she could see was Sharon wrapped in David's strong arms, her soft body pressed into the hardness of his.

'Caroline! Caroline!'

She heard her name with a curious sense of detachment and looked up to see David rushing across the headland toward her, his sandy hair flying wildly about his head.

'*No!*' The word was torn from her throat

and without thinking, she whirled and began to run. She didn't want to see him. She didn't want to hear his seductive voice again, look into his handsome face and know he could never be hers. The wind loosened tendrils of hair from her braid and ran clammy fingers down her spine. The cliff rose sharply in a rough and ill-defined and sometimes impassable footpath but she scrambled toward it anyway before suddenly being hit from behind and sent sprawling face down in a heavy heap on to the ground.

David had thrown his arms around her waist and tackled her.

'God in heaven!' he breathed roughly, falling on top of her. 'Are you trying to kill yourself? There's a twenty-foot drop on the other side of this cliff. Why did you keep on running?'

'Leave me alone!' she gasped into the dirt.

'Why? What have I done to make you run away from me?' He shifted his weight and forcibly turned her flat on her back, looking into her stricken eyes.

She closed them tightly and squirmed, trying to escape his hold but he held her fast, throwing one long leg across both of hers. He began to brush the dirt from her face but had to grab at her hands and hold them above her head on the ground when she instinctively started to claw at him. Straining against his hold, she continued to writhe and jerk beneath him, kicking in an effort to get away but the entire length of his warm heavy body held her down. No matter which way she moved, she couldn't shake off his touch.

He held her easily for long minutes fully conscious of the way her softly rounded curves were ineffectually thrusting against his solid immovable weight. He didn't try to stop her. Almost with complacence he kept still, letting her body rub up against his.

The warmth of his breath was fanning her face, stirring her, making her heart race and she redoubled her efforts to get away from him. An innate sensuality oozed from him and she was dangerously susceptible to it even now, even after everything that happened. She had to get away. She didn't want to be so near to him, to be tantalised by this sheer male magnetism that could never be hers. He was engaged to Sharon now and this was insanity. Her slender body arched in one last desperate attempt to throw him off.

'If you're doing this for my benefit,' his mouth curved in a sudden wicked grin, 'move your hips a little more to the left.'

She stopped instantly, a strangling gasp catching in her throat, a furious blush of mortification flooding her face when she realised just how provocative the movements were.

He knew he embarrassed her but he kept looking into her eyes steadily, without moving, before his breath was finally expelled in a harsh sigh. 'All right, Caro. What's this all about?' He let her hands go but didn't lever himself off her. 'You looked like death this morning when Sharon showed you her ring. Then you ran up to your room and locked yourself in. It couldn't have been that big a surprise to you, could it?'

She squeezed her eyes shut and turned her head away, trying to swallow back the bitterness rising in her throat. How dare he rub it in like that? 'No,' she said raggedly, her mouth twisting with self derision, 'it was no surprise. Deep down I expected it all along.'

'Then what's this all about?'

Rage and anger boiled in her and spilled over. He couldn't be *that* insensitive. 'Nothing!' she grated.

'Don't tell me, "nothing"!' he shouted back. 'It was enough to make you want to kill yourself. If I hadn't stopped you, you'd have thrown yourself off this cliff.'

Her head spun back to him and her eyes were huge and green and distended with something close to hatred. 'I would not!' she cried. 'You accused me of being suicidal once before. It wasn't true then. It isn't true now.'

'Then why are you always walking so bloody close to the edge?' The anger grating his voice matched the passionate fury in his eyes. 'Every time I see you walking out here I wonder if this'll be the time you "accidentally" lose your footing. I can't keep my mind on my work any more. You're making me a nervous wreck. The cattle—the crops—the hens—they're all suffering because of you. You're driving me crazy!'

Her eyes widened even more as disbelief ran through her. She became very still. 'Even if that was true,' she whispered, 'what's it to you, anyway?'

'What's it to me?' He looked astounded. 'Caroline! *Don't you know?*' It was a tortured question and he closed his eyes on a spasm of pain, suddenly losing control of emotions that had been bottled up too long. His mouth came down and ground against the parted softness of hers in a hot, hungry, punishing kiss that was unlike anything she ever expected from him. The hard probe of his tongue in her mouth suddenly made her heart leap, firing all her senses with a flame-like brilliance. His hands dug into her shoulders, her breasts, her waist, her hips, moulding her to his length as the fire between them began to rage out of control.

She spread her fingers against the bulging muscles of his shoulders, trying to wedge a space so she could breathe but the hardness of his chest was welded to hers and all she could feel was his hard masculinity crushing all the fight out of her. She became boneless and yielding and pliant beneath him. In spite of Sharon, this was what she wanted. Why should she fight it any more?'

She began to kiss him back with increasing passion, loving the heat and strength of his body on hers. Without thinking, her arms curled around him and dug into the shining thickness of his hair.

Sensing her complete surrender, the quality of his kiss changed, became gentle and seeking and drugging with a subtle mastery that wasn't there before. 'Oh, Caro, let me——'

'*What's going on here?*' The shocked sound of Grandy's voice intruded like a blast of icy wind.

David grew rigid, lifting his head and sucking in a long ragged breath before expelling it harshly in defeat. Rolling to his feet without a word, he extended a hand to help Caroline up.

Her face was brick red, her lips swollen, her hair wildly disordered. 'We fell,' she whispered shakily, self-consciously brushing herself down and straightening her shirt where it had come undone from the waistband of her jeans.

David squared his jaw and with a forceful lift of his head looked Grandy right in the eye. 'I tackled her,' he said dispassionately. 'I thought she was going to throw herself off the cliff.'

Dumbfounded, Grandy's mouth fell open.

'Throw herself—I don't believe it! She's been walking these cliffs since she was five years old. Why would she suddenly take it in her head to throw herself off them?'

'I don't know. That's what I was trying to find out.'

Grandy's eyes narrowed shrewdly. Studying this tall, still, giant of a man, he noted the white lines of strain at the sides of his mouth and the smouldering quality of his bright blue eyes. 'It looked to me like you were trying to find out something altogether different.'

Dull red colour ran up David's neck but he didn't say anything.

Grandy continued to look at him then dragged a distracted hand through his hair, painfully aware of the palpable constraint between these two. 'Steven came running to me and said his dad was chasing Caroline and maybe something was wrong. That's why I'm here.'

'Nothing was wrong,' Caroline said tightly before glancing angrily at David. She had herself in control again now. The insanity of the moment had passed. 'Mr Chivalry, here, just jumped to the wrong conclusion, that's all.'

'Why you——' David flared.

But Grandy interrupted him. 'That's enough, both of you.' He looked from one to the other and almost smiled at the way they didn't see him at all. They were intent only on glaring at each other. 'One lunatic in the house at a time is all I can stand. Sharon's enough to drive me up a wall with that engagement ring of hers. I don't need you two quarrelling as well. Settle your differences and then come home.' He turned and began to make his way back to smoother ground when he met Steven and Tim running to him with the dog nipping at their heels.

'Down, Ruff,' he shouted over the excited barks. 'It's nothing to worry about boys. Nothing's wrong. It wasn't what you thought you saw. Come along.' He whistled for the dog and put an arm out to shepherd the boys home.

Steven evaded his outstretched hand and looked at his father and then at Caroline with big solemn eyes.

'It's all right, Steve,' David said evenly. 'Go with Grandy. Caroline and I will be there shortly.' He watched him turn and run to catch up to the others then he looked at Caroline and let out a long slow breath. 'I'm sorry,' he said. 'I was stupid.'

'No. The stupidity isn't yours, David. It's mine. All mine.' She hugged her arms around herself and shivered, swallowing back a choking feeling. Ever since he'd appeared on their doorstep, she'd been throwing herself at him, weaving her dreams around him, making him the centre of her existence. How could she blame him for taking what she offered? Sick despair overwhelmed her.

She started to turn away but he reached out and put a hand on her wrist to detain her. 'Don't go,' he said bleakly. 'Not until we've talked. I've hurt you and I never wanted that to happen.' His deeply blue eyes were intent with anguish.

She looked at him and never felt so utterly miserable in all her life. She couldn't have his love. She wouldn't tolerate his pity. Jerking her hand away, she moved past him and threw a look back over her shoulder. 'I'm sure I'll get over it.'

David sighed in defeat and without another word watched her pick her way back down the cliff path until she became a moving blur on the horizon.

Dinner that evening was a disaster. Grandy scowled at the roast Caroline had burnt and muttered darkly when he passed the bowl of lumpy mashed potatoes to Sharon. He had to clear his throat several times to get her attention, she was so engrossed in her left hand with the new engagement ring on it. Exasperation was written all over his face when he watched Caroline and David push their food around their plates in silence, not even making a pretence of eating. When Tim and Rob began to squabble over whose turn it was to gather eggs the next day, Grandy slammed his hands on the table and bellowed at all of them.

'I want all your differences settled here and now. Or I'll take each one of you out behind the barn and give you a thrashing you'll not soon forget.'

David's eyes lifted slowly to look at him with disconcerting directness.

'That means you as well, David,' he sputtered. 'As long as you're living here, you'll be treated as one of my grandsons—answerable to me.'

He sounded close to losing his temper and all at once Caroline snapped out of her apathy, becoming alarmed at the sickly grey colour running into his face. He looked ready to have another stroke and she, more than anybody, knew how necessary it was for him not to have any stress or worry. 'All right, Grandy. Don't get upset. Tim, Rob, no more taking turns. You'll both gather the eggs together from now on.' Helping Grandy up from his chair, she murmured soothingly, leading him into the sitting room. 'I'll bring you a nice cup of tea. Just sit here and relax.'

He suffered her ministrations a minute more then roughly pulled his arm away and settled down in his chair by himself. 'Stop fussing,' he growled. 'I'm not an old woman who needs to be mollycoddled. Get back in that kitchen and settle things between you and David. I don't want a repeat of tonight's fiasco ever again.'

'I'm sorry about that,' she said, her lips quivering. 'But there's nothing to settle.' Her eyes met his squarely and suddenly brimmed with stubborn green sparks. 'I might as well tell you now. I'm leaving, Grandy. Just as soon as Daddy and Morwenna get back, I'm going to Penzance to look for a job.'

His mouth twisted in derision. 'Well, well, well. Isn't that just great?' A sneer ran over his face. 'I'll tell you the same thing I told David: running away isn't going to solve a thing. You both ought to have your heads examined.'

Her jaw started to drop in confusion. 'You told David——?'

'You think you're the only one to come up with the bright idea of running away instead of talking things out? But at least he's not high-tailing it as far as Penzance,' he said scathingly. 'While you were burning the roast, he told me to start looking for someone else to help me with the farmwork. Tomorrow he's moving back to Morwenna's.'

Her breath was drawn in harshly but she couldn't say a word. He didn't have to leave because of her. Then she thought maybe it was just a coincidence. Now that he and Sharon were engaged, it wouldn't look right for him to be staying here under the same roof. That's probably all it was: a matter of propriety.

Grandy's voice was rich with disgust, breaking into her thoughts. 'In my day there wasn't all this pussyfooting around. When I met your grandmother, I fell head over heels in love with her and I told her so. What's wrong with you two?'

'Oh, Grandy, things aren't so simple these days——'

'Don't hand me that. Love is love no matter what generation it's in.'

She was quiet for a moment then she gave a little sigh. 'I don't know anything about love. Besides, there's Sharon——'

'That scatterbrain! But at least she's honest with her emotions. She doesn't try to put on a brave front and pretend everything's all right when everything's upside down. The way you and David were at supper was enough to give a cast iron stomach indigestion. Now go on, get out there and settle things.'

Caroline compressed her lips and did as she was told but the only one in the kitchen was Steven, silently clearing the table. There was no reproach in his eyes when he looked up and saw her. He simply went on with what he was doing and then he helped her dry the dishes and put them away. She didn't ask him where his father was. She knew he was most likely off somewhere with Sharon and she wasn't that much of a masochist that she had to hear him say it. They worked together in silence and when they were done, Steven gave her a solemn smile and left the room without a word.

Later she realised it was the silence that was beginning to grate on her nerves. It wasn't soothing. It was full of a seething tension. The clocks had crept past midnight long ago and she still wasn't able to sleep. Pacing her floor in her room, restless and miserable, her heart thudding, she was full of futile yearnings she couldn't master. David was out of reach, so why didn't she just accept it and put him out of her mind? But no, all she could think of was how only a wall separated them. He was lying there on the other side of it in his own narrow bed, so near yet so far. She wondered if he was asleep or if he, too, was restless and strung up. Every time she closed her eyes, she pictured his handsome craggy face. Everything about him from the clean male smell of him to the glorious feel of his mouth on hers to the velvety sound of his voice returned to assault her senses. He was an obsession she had to overcome. He wasn't hers to love.

Her restless pacing carried her to the shadowy hallway, heading for the bathroom, intending to splash cold water in her face to rid herself of this fever in her blood. But halfway down the hall, she stopped hearing the sound of muffled sobbing coming from behind Tim's door. Another nightmare? Why not? There was enough tension in this house to trigger off anything. But she thought Tim was over them now since Steven had come to share his room.

Pushing open his door, she peered through the gloom and saw Tim sound asleep in his bed. Quickly turning to the other bed, she saw Steven on his side, his blanket bunched around his face.

'Steve,' she said softly, 'what's wrong?'

He didn't answer her.

'Please tell me.' She sat on the edge of his bed and gently rubbed his shoulder.

He shuddered helplessly for a minute then launched himself into her arms, sobbing incoherently into her neck.

'Oh darling, it's all right. I'm here,' she soothed over and over, rocking him back and forth.

After a while he hiccupped back his sobs and wiped his eyes. 'Did I wake up Tim?'

'No,' she said quietly. 'But we might. Come with me.'

Leading him to her room, she settled him in her bed and sat on the edge of it beside him, smiling a baffled smile into his solemn, tear-wet eyes, waiting. If it took all night, she'd find out what was troubling him.

He dragged his eyes away from her and

looked around the small uncluttered room without any expression. There were unadorned white walls and a polished wood floor that was bare except for a small round white rug. Ruffled white curtains moved at the open window in the gentle night-time breeze. There was a low dresser with an oblong mirror against one wall and this narrow bed with its delicately embroidered white candlewick spread against the other. It was nothing like any of the other bedrooms with their colourful decor. The boys had pop art posters covering their walls and Sharon's room was plastered with pictures of movie stars. Caroline's room was a haven of austere simplicity.

Steven looked at her again and his eyes filled with easy tears. 'My dad says we can't live here with you any more.'

Somehow she wasn't surprised. 'Oh, Steve.' Her heart went out to him. 'It's just for a little while,' she soothed. 'When your dad gets married, if he doesn't come back here to live, he'll at least bring you round for visits. You know that, don't you? You'll be able to see us all the time.'

If he heard her, he gave no indication of it. He burrowed his face into her chest desperately.

'Don't upset yourself for nothing, darling. I'll always love you. You don't have to worry about that ever changing. No matter where you go or what you do, you'll always be special to me.'

He merely clung tighter, his tears dampening the front of her nightgown, and Caroline felt more and more helpless. All she could do was hold him tightly and make soothing noises and tell him over and over how much she loved him. After a while she felt him relax against her and she knew somehow he had fallen asleep in her arms.

Looking down into his blotchy face, she had to wonder what kind of mother Sharon was going to make for him. When she and David had children of their own, would she go out of her way to include him and not make him feel he was an outsider? A pang struck at her and she smoothed his dark hair away from his eyes. 'Dear little boy,' she whispered fiercely, 'no one will ever slight you. Not as long as you have me for an aunt!'

A soft footfall sounded in the hall and Caroline gently lowered him back on her pillow and covered him and quietly tiptoed away. Just as she pulled open her door, she saw David standing there, his hand poised ready to knock. 'Oh!' she gasped.

'Sorry. I'm looking for Steven. He's not in his bed.'

'He's here with me,' she whispered, pulling the door open further and standing out of the way so he could see into the room.

Looking past her to his sleeping son, he breathed deeply then looked down into her reddening face as she tried to drag her eyes away from him.

He was wearing nothing but a pair of jeans and the width of his naked chest made her weak. Some men had hairy chests, she knew from reading about the different heroes in the books she borrowed from the library, but David's skin was smooth and tanned and rippling with wide bunching muscles. For one wild moment she had the insane urge to press herself against him to savour the feel of that powerful body against hers. She kept looking at him, drawn to the rugged symmetry of his chest and arms, the fluid graceful beauty of his body. She had touched him once before, delighting in the feel of his skin against hers. She wanted to touch him again. Oh, how she wanted . . .

'Steven was having a bad time,' she said quickly, nervously rushing into speech, stepping into the hall and pulling the door behind her with shaking hands. 'Er—he's afraid he won't see any of us again once you leave.' Her eyes darted everywhere but at him.

'I see.' He expelled a harsh breath. 'I'm sorry he bothered you.'

'He didn't. I was awake anyway.' The minute she said that she could have bitten out her tongue. He probably knew he was the cause of her sleeplessness.

'Caroline——'

'No! Don't say anything!' She turned away but he put his hands on her shoulders, pulling her back against him. She could feel the warmth of his breath stirring her hair and closed her eyes in despair. How could she want him like this when he belonged to her sister?

'I don't want to leave tomorrow with things the way they are between us. I have to talk to you.'

'We have nothing to say——' she began but all her breath suddenly left her in a rush when David bent his head and let his lips nuzzle the side of her neck.

Every other thought in her mind fled. Her bones melted. Right or wrong meant nothing now. She was only aware of a blissful heady sensation where nothing else mattered but that she stay here close and safe in his arms. His hands circled her slender waist and slid up her ribcage to cup her breasts, feeling them straining against the soft material of her nightgown, swelling, hardening in his palms. Her breath became panting and her head swam dizzily when he turned her in his arms to face him, his mouth finding hers in a warm and gentle and devastatingly sensual caress. Raining kisses over her eyes, nose, cheeks, ears and neck, he claimed her lips again with hungry possession.

Her heart was pounding, her hands curling into the warm bare skin of his chest where she could feel his heart hammering against them.

'*What's going on here?*' Once again, the shock in Grandy's indrawn whisper ripped them apart.

It was three o'clock in the morning and they were standing in the darkened hallway outside her door in each other's arms, she in a dishevelled nightgown and unbuttoned robe, he barefoot, wearing only jeans. No one could blame Grandy for jumping to the obvious conclusion.

CHAPTER NINE

THEY all kept staring at one another in stunned silence. Grandy's jaw dropped open incredulously. His face was slowly becoming the colour of lead. His chest rose and fell in struggling gasps and he began to tremble and had to lean back against the wall as if it was too much of an effort to stand upright without something to support him. His eyes were wide and distended, moving from Caroline to David and back again. Then he looked balefully at David and his face changed as a wild rage ran through him. 'You have compromised my granddaughter, sir,' he said in a hoarse, unrecognisable voice.

Caroline looked at him, transfixed, not believing what she was hearing. It was such bad melodrama. No one talked like that in this day and age. Even Grandy's generation never talked like that. She glanced at David who was as stunned as herself. 'No!' she said, her head jerking from side to side in horrified denial.

Grandy didn't even see her. He managed to push himself away from the wall and stand upright, swaying, his fists clenched. His eyes were filling his face, pinning David with a menacing glare. 'What are you going to do about it?'

David didn't answer. He faced him squarely, without flinching, his mouth thinning to a sick bluish line in his darkening face.

'Well?' Grandy's whole stance was full of wrath.

After a moment, David closed his eyes and his head snapped back as if something was suddenly released in him. His mouth curved upward and he laughed a strangely mournful laugh and Caroline could see the shine of his teeth in the dimness. 'I'll do the honourable thing, of course,' he said quietly, as if it was a foregone conclusion. 'I will marry her.'

Caroline's mouth fell open on a faint gasp. '*No!*'

Grandy advanced on her, filling the hallway. His dark face was contorted and twisted and his eyes were terrible. 'You will go to your room, Caroline!'

'No! It's not what you're thinking. David and I were just——'

His hand snaked out, slashing his bony fingers across her face, making her stagger backwards. She would have fallen if David hadn't reached out and caught her in time. She didn't cry out or look away from Grandy. Her eyes were locked with his then after a moment her face turned from surprised horror to a look of deep and profound sorrow.

David kept his arm around her and watched the imprint of a hand redden on her cheek. His jaw hardened when he turned and glared back at Grandy. 'That was uncalled for,' he said in a livid, shaking voice. 'I'll marry your granddaughter as soon as it can be arranged but don't you dare ever hit her again or you'll have to answer to me!'

Grandy stepped back from him as if coming out of a daze and smiled drearily, turning, almost staggering in the direction of the bathroom.

David slowly let out the breath he was holding and looked down at Caroline's stricken face and pressed her to his side reassuringly. 'We'll talk in the morning. Right now, I'll get Steve and leave you to your privacy.'

'No. He's all right,' she argued in a small shaky voice. 'Don't wake him. I wouldn't sleep anyway.'

'You're not to worry about a thing.'

A small sob escaped her, choking off any retort she might have made.

'Caroline, everything will be all right,' he said firmly, tightening his arm around her. Something stirred in the depths of his eyes and her heart jerked ridiculously. 'Your grandfather was shocked by what he thought he saw, that's all. Just remember he's a sick man who has to be humoured for now. Leave everything to me. We'll sort it all out in the morning.' He dropped a gentle kiss on her hair and gave her a small reluctant push towards her room.

By morning, she knew nothing could make things right again. In the grey light of dawn, she saw David's lonely figure crossing the paddock on his way to the barn to begin the milking. There was something particularly moving about the sight of him walking alone like that. The rest of the house was beginning to stir and she turned from her silent vigil at the window and bleakly looked at Steven's rosy face on her pillow. There was no reason for any of them to be alone again. But she couldn't go through with it. She just couldn't.

Steven's bright eyes opened without any sign of confusion and he smiled at her. It was a sad smile, one far beyond his years, making her heart go out to him.

'Good morning, Steve. Did you sleep?'

He nodded and pushed back the sheet and bounded over to her, 'I love you, Caro,' he said fiercely, throwing himself into her arms with his eyes closed tightly.

'Oh, darling, I love you too.'

'I wish I could always stay with you. I wish you were my mother.'

She sighed, hugging him, swamped with a bitter ambivalence. If she said nothing and let what happened last night stand, David would marry her and she'd be Steven's mother and his joy would be complete. So would hers. But it was unfair to find her happiness at someone else's expense. Even if there wasn't Sharon to consider, she couldn't allow Grandy to force David to marry her. She remembered the look on David's face and the way he laughed when he said he'd do the honourable thing. It had to be the terrible irony of the situation that made him laugh. He had to remember another time, another place, with Judith's father most likely confronting him in the same way. Another deep sigh came from her. Poor David. He didn't deserve such treatment when his only crime was being the steady rock for a lonely woman to cling to. What a mess she'd made of everything. By loving him, she ruined everything for him.

Pulling herself together with an effort, she smiled brightly at Steven and gently patted his back. 'Time to get washed and brushed and see what today might bring. Do you want to use the bathroom first, or shall I?'

The briskness in her tone was hard to sustain but somehow she managed to get through breakfast without making her distress obvious to Sharon and her brothers.

The boys were outside playing and it was early afternoon before David and Grandy emerged from the cubbyhole off the living room they called Grandy's study. David's face was expressionless, set in deliberate lines and Grandy's was flushed and triumphant. Caroline had been sitting in a chair with her hands folded in her lap, waiting, and when she saw their faces, her heart sank. Somehow she got to her feet and stood before them rigid and motionless.

'I told Grandy I didn't think you'd want a big wedding since your family just had one,' David said stiffly. 'A simple ceremony would be best, don't you agree?'

She tried to read his face but its impassive lines told her nothing. She sensed a deep anger and bitterness in him as if he regarded her with contempt and himself with disgust. A confused wariness trembled through her but she dimissed it at once. He had to be saying this for Grandy's benefit. He didn't really plan to go through with it. She glanced at Grandy's smug face then looked at David again, pausing, her frown becoming troubled. 'Yes,' she hesitated, 'a simple ceremony.'

His face was grim for a minute then he nodded curtly as if he hadn't expected her to say anything else and turned on his heel, striding to the door and flinging it open without another word.

It closed behind him with ominous silence and for a long second Grandy stood watching her then he laughed, letting out an explosive breath. 'Don't look so tragic, girl. You should be on top of the world right now. I've just landed you the biggest fish in the pond.'

Caroline stiffened then looked at him in amazement. 'What! You mean you planned this whole thing?'

'Planned? What planned? I merely saw an opportunity I couldn't pass up.'

'Grandy!' She was horrified. 'You can't do this!'

'After you've thought about it for a while, you'll thank me.'

'But you're forcing David to marry me! I can't let you do that. You know there was nothing between us last night. At least nothing compromising. He kissed me, that's all. And you know it.'

'Yes, I know. You're both too moral to abuse the time and the place never mind the inclination.'

'Then, why?'

'It's time for you to be married, Caroline. That's why. And what better man than David? You love him. I'm sure he feels the same way about you if the kiss I saw was anything to go by.'

Her face flamed. 'Oh, Grandy, don't you understand? What girl wants a husband who has to be forced to marry her? Besides, what about Sharon?'

'Sharon?' He lifted his shoulders and spread his hands in exasperation. 'What's she got to do with it? You saw the way she rushed out of here this morning without even stopping to wish you well. She barely tasted her breakfast. Her head's full of air. She can't think of anything or anybody but J——'

'Caroline! *Caroline!*' Steven squealed, running in from the kitchen and throwing himself at her. 'Sharon just came home and she told me you're going to marry Daddy and be my mother!'

Her arms helplessly closed around him and all her breath left her. She looked accusingly at Grandy. 'Who told *her*?'

'I did.' His smile was smug. 'Early this morning while you were busy getting breakfast.'

Blank disbelief twisted her mouth. 'Why?'

'So you and David couldn't back out.' He grinned, looking as if he was waiting to be congratulated for this master stroke of planning.

'I don't believe it! How did she take it?'

'She's very happy for you.'

Caroline stared at him with the feeling she was becoming lost in a slippery wet fog. It didn't make sense. How could he be so unthinkingly cruel? And how could Sharon be so magnanimous? As flighty as she was, a broken engagement had to make her desolate not happy. This had to hurt her. Sharon loved David. She'd talked of nothing else since the first day he came here. 'Oh,

Grandy, don't you realise what a mess you've made of everything?'

'I've made?' His eyes blithely twinkled with mischief. 'I'm just a helpless old man who's had a stroke. You'd better be careful I don't get upset and have another.'

Her confusion was complete now. He wasn't one bit concerned that he'd meddled in all their lives. 'It would serve you right if you did,' she muttered.

His bushy white eyebrows rose in mock surprise. 'You're getting cheeky, young lady. I know you don't really mean it so I'll forgive you this time but you'd better be more careful in future—especially in front of your son.' He ruffled Steven's hair and grinned at him. 'If Caro's going to be your mother, she should set a good example, don't you think?'

Steven clung tightly to her and beamed at him from the safe haven of her arms. 'My mom,' he said almost reverently.

Caroline held him, quivering, knowing deep in her heart it wouldn't come to that. It couldn't.

Her first impulse was to wait and see what David had to say but the more she thought about it, the more disturbed she became. She kept remembering the look on his face when he came out of Grandy's study. She'd never seen him quite so grim before. It was as if he blamed her for what happened. Taking her courage in both hands, she went outside to find him.

He was behind the barn tinkering with the tractor. His shirt was off and his sinewy back muscles were glistening with sweat as he bent over the engine. Caroline bunched her hands in the pockets of her jeans, trying to ignore the mad thumping of her heart at the sight of all that warm naked skin. She cleared her throat awkwardly trying to find the right thing to say.

'David?'

He glanced back over his shoulder and, seeing it was her, wiped his forehead with the back of his arm and turned back to the motor tightening a bolt with a wrench. 'Yes?'

'I have to talk to you,' she said shakily.

'Talk away.' He didn't stop what he was doing.

A mounting frustration made her voice wobble. 'I can't talk to your back.'

'There's really nothing more to be said. Your grandfather's making all the arrangements. You'll have to see him to discuss your plans. We'll be married in the next day or so, he told me.'

'No!'

'It's done, Caroline. You got what you wanted. Now leave me in peace.'

'What *I* wanted?' She was flabbergasted. 'It takes two, you know. I didn't plan to have Grandy pull the outraged father act, if that's what you're thinking.'

He threw a sarcastic look over his shoulder then turned back and gave the wrench a vicious turn.

A sudden white hot anger ran through her, making her rigid. She grabbed at his arm and pulled him around to face her. 'My God, that's it, isn't it?' she railed, yelping when the wrench slipped from his grasp and struck her foot. Pain shot through her but it was nothing compared to the pain in her heart. 'You think *I* did it! It was Grandy's doing, not mine,' she choked, hopping on one foot and blinking back the sharp sting of tears. 'I don't want to marry you any more than you want to marry me.'

'We no longer have a choice. Your grandfather made that clear.' He knelt down in front of her and took her foot in his hand, forcibly holding her still, removing her shoe and running gentle fingers over her instep. 'It's not broken but you're going to have a bruise.'

'I don't care about my foot!' she gasped as the pain throbbed through it. 'My grandfather's wrong. You do have a choice. You were married once under a cloud of gossip and suspicion. I'm not going to let it happen again. Not with me. Besides, there's Sharon. You can tell her it was all a misunderstanding. Go ahead and marry each other. I'll wish you well. I'll even dance at your wedding!' Uncontrollable tears began streaming down her face. In her humiliation, she only hoped David thought it was because of her foot.

He slowly straightened and looked straight into her face with speechless shock. They were standing close together, intensely aware of each other, then he made an eloquent gesture with his shoulders and the grim twist of his mouth softened in spite of himself. 'What's that supposed to mean?" he asked quietly. 'Sharon's engaged to John. I don't think you're going to do much walking for the next couple of days, let alone dancing.'

Her jaw dropped. Ignoring her foot, she stared at him. 'John? John *Polgearon*? What are you saying? How can she be engaged to him? You were kissing her. I saw you. When she showed me the ring you gave her, she was in your arms. Her lipstick was all over you. And you both looked so . . .' her voice faded away to almost nothing, '. . . happy.'

His eyes widened then suddenly narrowed to tiny blue pinpoints. A breathless stillness held him. Something moved in his face. 'That's what you meant when you said you remembered who I was,' he murmured to himself. A suggestion of a smile curved his mouth. 'You came in when I was congratulating Sharon,' he said softly. 'You said you thought you heard John's car on the drive. And you did. He'd bought the ring that morning but couldn't wait to give it to her. He proposed then had to get back to work.'

Her shoulders slumped and all her breath left her in a noisy rush. She felt stupid yet at the same time unbearably relieved. 'I thought . . .' Sudden colour poured into her face when she remembered her reaction to Sharon's engagement. From the dawning comprehension on David's face, she knew he was remembering it too. Humiliation swept through her. Everything he needed to know was staring him in the face. But she couldn't allow that. Her pride had her scuttling for cover. 'Well, that's one less thing to worry about,' she said with a husky quiver. 'I'm glad Sharon isn't going to be hurt by all this. But I mean it when I say you don't have to go through with Grandy's grand plan. We won't be marrying, David. In spite of what he says. He may be as stubborn as a mule but you haven't met stubborn until you've come up against me.'

David's expression darkened. 'That I can believe.'

She turned on her heel and hobbled out.

Two days later Caroline and Grandy were still at an impasse when a deliriously happy Morwenna and Alec came home from their honeymoon. They were brought down to earth with a bump when they found out what happened in their absence and realised

Caroline wouldn't back down from her stand.

'I kept telling your father something was wrong,' Morwenna said quietly. 'That's why we cut our trip short. How can you even contemplate such an idea?' She stared in shocked disbelief, watching her pack her suitcase. It was midnight and everyone else was sleeping in the big rambling farmhouse. 'I thought you loved David. You can't leave in the middle of the night like this. The wedding's set for tomorrow. Why, you'll be leaving him standing at the altar!'

A laugh suspiciously like a sob sounded deep in Caroline's throat. 'It's hardly going to come to that. When David gets up in the morning, I'll be gone. He won't make it as far as the church.'

'You're too late, Caro. Grandy told Mrs Trerhyn yesterday. By tomorrow morning, it'll be all over the village. You, of all people, couldn't do that to him. Please, for your own sake as well as his, marry him. If you don't, neither of you will ever be happy.'

'Oh Morwenna, you don't know. You don't know.'

'I know a lot more than you think I do. Grandy was wrong, I'll grant you that. He never should have tried to force you into this but it's just his impatience, that's all. He was tired of watching the two of you pretend you weren't in love with each other. Forgive an old man his foibles and simply look at the good that's coming out of it all. David will have the loving wife he needs and Steven will have the mother he was meant to have.' Her mouth shook. 'He's yours, Caro, more than you'll ever know. He should have been yours a long time ago.'

'No. Don't say that. Oh, don't you see how wrong this is? David thinks I'm behind the whole thing. He thinks I had to resort to force to get a husband. I told him I had nothing to do with it but he doesn't believe me. He's had one shotgun marriage already. I love him too much to force him into another.' She went on relentlessly folding the clothes and stuffing them into her suitcase. 'I can't do that to him. I've got two choices: to stay and marry him and hurt him, or to leave and hurt him. This way, when I leave, he'll be hurt less.'

Morwenna heaved a sigh and resigned herself to a long sleepless night. It was useless to keep arguing when Caroline closed her mind to reason but she kept it up until two o'clock before giving in and going back to bed. 'You know I only hope you'll be happy wherever you go,' she said finally, with a long-suffering sigh. 'Let me hear from you, won't you?'

'Of course.' Caroline smiled sadly. 'I'll be all right. After a while you'll see this is for the best.'

The night was slowly passing and Caroline

took her time writing a note of explanation for Grandy. His health was much improved so she didn't really think her leaving would cause him to have another stroke. He knew she wouldn't be forced into this marriage. She'd told him often enough in the past two days. He also knew how stubborn she could be so it wouldn't be any surprise. David was another matter. There was really nothing she could say to him so after an hour, she gave up trying. Propping Grandy's note against her pillow, she glanced around her room one last time then quietly slipped out.

She stopped at Tim's door and looked in on him and Steven but quickly closed it and bit back a sob. Steven was almost her son. Almost.

That was the story of her life, she thought with a pang of snivelling self pity. Almost a bride, almost a wife, almost a mother . . .

CHAPTER TEN

EVERYTHING was dark and still when Caroline hobbled down the darkened path some distance from her house. The swelling in her foot had lessened and now she was left with only a dull ache whenever she put pressure on it. She hoped her heart would heal as fast. This was the last time she'd be able to wander aimlessly on the cliffs like this and listen to the soothing rhythm of the sea. The night breeze drifted past her, carrying the unmistakable scent of seaweed. It gently lifted her hair away from her face and carved her flowered voile dress to the slender curves of her body.

She shifted her suitcase to her other hand, sighing restlessly. In a little while she'd be in Penzance and it would be the beginning of a whole new life for her. If she couldn't find work there, maybe she'd try to venture as far as London. Her favourite author always made it sound like such an exciting place in many of her books. Girls were always going there, combining their resources and sharing flats and bedsitters and making a go of it. They even fell in love and found their happily ever afters. Nothing said it only had to happen in fiction. She could try her luck there in real life as well.

If she began to think of how much she'd miss her family and this slower paced part of the country, she resolutely put it out of her mind. It was time to go on, time for a change. She'd allow herself no regrets. She told herself that eventually she'd be able to think of David and Steven without this sick misery tearing her to pieces.

The sky was beginning to blaze on the horizon, the darkness rapidly giving way to glorious hues of pink and gold and violet. Caroline stopped and set her case down in the blowing grass and stood watching the sun slowly rise in a spectacular silent burst of glory from the water's far distant edge.

'Beautiful, isn't it? But it's too silent. At the very least, such splendour should have a crashing symphony orchestra accompanying it.'

They were her thoughts exactly but she hadn't voiced them.

Stiffening, she whirled around with a sudden jerk and looked up into David's handsome face. He was standing behind her dressed in a dark business suit and looking very much at ease. She began to tremble and tried to look away but his bright blue eyes caught and held hers and she couldn't move. The gentle line of his mouth curved in a warm smile, making her weak with the sudden longing to throw herself into his arms. She could actually feel every nerve ending screaming to reach out and put her hands on his tall pulsing body. The clean warm scent of him was all around her, driving her mad. How could she feel this way? She was running away from him, for heaven's sake. A sudden mindless heat and embarrassment swept through her.

David's smile deepened knowingly before he tore his eyes away from her and bent down to pick up her case, gesturing for her to continue walking in the same direction she had been going. 'May I walk a little of the way with you?' he asked huskily, completely throwing her into a panic. She expected him to be angry, not gentle. Why wasn't he forcing her to turn around and go back? She hesitated, not knowing what to do, and her legs began to quiver into a painful stiff awkwardness.

He smiled again, more gently this time, and she nearly burst into tears. 'Caroline?'

She swallowed and forced her gangly legs to move.

At her first hobbling step, he put out an impersonal hand and caught her elbow in his warm gentle grip. 'Is your foot hurting you?'

Her whole arm seemed to flame when he touched her and she didn't even know she had a foot. Her attention was forced to the rocky sloping path in a struggling attempt to appear indifferent and aloof and self sufficient but her pulse was pounding wildly, giving her away. 'It's not hurting really,' she whispered jerkily. 'Just a little tender when I walk on it.'

He nodded and they went on together in silence. It was an awkward silence but Caroline couldn't seem to break it. How did she deal with him? She wished she knew what he was thinking. His face was set in impassive but pleasant lines that told her nothing. The lack of expression only made her heart beat faster.

Warily watching him sideways through her lashes, she tried not to be drawn to him but his nearness brought a warm rush of feeling sweeping through her. Lots of men had sand-coloured hair and thick winged brows but why did his nose have to have that fascinating bump on the bridge of it? Or his cheeks those deep slashing grooves? Or his mouth such a definite slant of sensuality? Tremors of longing shook her when she added up all his features to this handsome wholeness that she had to resist.

He moved easily beside her, his long loping strides shortened to keep pace with her. He didn't remove his hand from her elbow and with a subtle pressure, he was letting her lean more and more of her weight on him.

They could have been two lovers walking hand in hand watching the sunrise. Only she was on her way out of his life and he had her case in one hand and her elbow in the other and the silence between them was awkward not companionable. She couldn't relax. Everything about him made her overcharged emotions tingle with breathless awareness. She began to falter, struggling with everything churning inside her. Vague confusion began to crystallise into outright pain.

The wind whipped at her hair when she stopped and turned to look him full in the face. Her shimmering green eyes were glazed with hurt. 'Why are you here, David?'

He didn't seem surprised by her question. Glancing sideways, he made a helpless little movement with his mouth before setting her case on the ground and turning to her, reaching out to brush back the hair blowing in her face, becoming wholly absorbed in the task. His touch was a caress, over and over again. His eyes ran over her face as if memorising every feature. 'It took me all my life to find you,' he said bleakly. 'How could I let you leave me?'

Unexpected tears welled up in her eyes. She couldn't utter a sound.

'No one ever loved me before,' he murmured, his fingers moving to smooth the blowing neckline of her dress. 'I was needed but never loved.'

'Morwenna told——'

'No,' he cut in gently. 'Morwenna didn't

have to tell me. You told me yourself. With everything but words.' His hands strayed to her neck, lightly curling into the long warm curve and his voice sank to a whisper. 'And I was telling you I love you with every kiss we shared, every look, every touch.'

Caroline struggled for composure, desperately trying not to listen to the passion throbbing in his voice. He was standing so close she could feel the heat of his body and smell his clean earthy scent. His breath stirred her hair, making her shiver. Why did he have to say this now? How was she ever going to live without him after hearing him say he loved her? She swallowed jerkily.

'I couldn't understand why you kept turning hot and cold,' he went on. 'When you were in my arms, you were so full of passion. I was sure you loved me. But whenever you were with your family, you could barely stand to look at me. And then that one time when we were so close, you pulled away and said you remembered who I was.'

'Oh, David,' she choked, 'I thought——'

He laughed softly and bent his head, helplessly burying his mouth in the side of her neck where her pulse beat wildly. His lips pushed the soft material of her dress aside and lightly rubbed against the creamy texture of her shoulder. His restless hands idly caressed the long pliant length of her spine, pulling her closer. 'Yes, my love, I finally realised what you thought—when you said you were going to dance at my wedding. But I never loved Sharon.'

She could feel his heart pounding heavily under the hand she convulsively pressed to his chest and when he raised his head she saw grave blue eyes glittering in his face.

'I was afraid it was something totally different,' he murmured.

A frown creased her forehead at the strangeness of his expression and she leaned back to put a little distance between them. 'What else could there be?'

His arms fell away from her and dropped defeatedly to his sides. She noticed the sudden involuntary clenching of his fists when he deliberately took a step away from her. 'I almost asked you several times to marry me,' he said tautly, looking out to the restlessly moving water at his side, 'but in the end, I couldn't. It wasn't time yet. I had to wait. I was torn between you and Steven. I didn't want to lose either of you.'

'Steven?' Her eyes became huge. What had Steven to do with it? He'd already told her about not being his real father. He knew it didn't make any difference to her.

'That's why I was so angry when your grandfather told me you deliberately led me into compromising situations so I would have to marry you,' he said unsteadily. 'You were forcing me to choose when there could be no choice.'

'But Grandy lied to you,' she whispered, her lips white and shaking. 'I never planned any of those moments together. He saw us by his accident, not my design.'

'I know. He finally admitted as much to me yesterday. His conscience was bothering him and he told me it was all his doing. I think deep down I knew it all along. I was hateful to you but I was more angry with myself. I didn't know what to do. And then I heard you leave this morning and I knew I had to come after you. You're my life, Caroline. Without you, there's no meaning to it.'

She watched all the colour slowly leave his face and a sudden shiver ran down her spine. A sense of foreboding seemed to fill the air about them and little darting thrills shot through her arms and legs and made the hair at the back of her neck stand on end. She had the strangest impulse to cry. 'But why?' she asked in a wobbly voice. 'Why would you have to choose between Steven and me? You told me you aren't his real father but that doesn't make any difference to the way I feel about him. Why do you think you can't have us both?'

He looked at her sombrely for a long minute and his mouth moved as if he wanted to say something but he couldn't force the words out. He closed his eyes on a spasm of pain and abruptly turned away, violently pounding one fist into the other. 'Oh, God!' he muttered grimly.

And then quite suddenly she knew.

Like a blinding light abruptly flooding a darkened room, she understood what it was that was so familiar about Steven. All of a sudden she could see it. Certain little mannerisms, the lift of his head, the flash of a smile, the lilting cadence in his voice, all of them were Philip Tregenna's.

Her mouth lost its pale flush and became as hard and fixed as stone. The emerald green of her eyes was the only colour in her face. Even the wind seemed to die down and the crashing sound of the waves beating against the rocks lessened. She stood beside him tall and white and still, alone and untouchable, with utter calm. The knowledge didn't wound her as once it might have done. She hadn't really loved Philip so all she could feel was a profound pity for him. She was more surprised at David's reluctance to tell her.

'You should have told me, David,' she said quietly, standing there in inflexible stillness. 'Steven is Philip Tregenna's son, isn't he?'

David was the image of shattered astonishment. Hardly breathing, not moving, he stared incredulously with wide blue eyes. '*You knew?*'

'No, but I should have done. I'm more

surprised that you found it so hard to tell me. I almost stumbled on it the day you told me why you married Judith. Why didn't you tell me then? It would have been the perfect time.'

He looked at her for a long leaden moment and his expression saddened. 'I didn't know then. I suspected as much but all I knew for sure was that you loved Philip and you didn't know he and Judith might have been lovers. I couldn't hurt you by telling you that.'

Her heart twisted. 'I only thought I loved him,' she cried. 'But I didn't. I didn't love him at all! I only thought I did. I let him ruin my life because I thought love had betrayed me. Is it such an elusive mystery that a person can't really tell if it's real or not?'

'Yes,' he murmured passionately. 'That's one of the things that makes it so tantalising and so wretched.'

She looked at him in caught out surprise. He knew. He understood everything she was feeling. Thin shards of ice trickled down her spine. How could he always be walking around in her mind like that? 'You said you didn't find out about Philip until yesterday. How——?'

He heaved a small sigh. 'Sir James rang me when Mrs Trerhyn told him we were getting married. I went and saw him last night.'

She unconsciously held her breath.

'He always blamed me for ruining Judith's

life,' he said dispassionately, 'and I never denied it. Maybe I should have done something different when she came to me and asked for help. Maybe I shouldn't have made it so easy for her. Maybe I should have made her talk to her father or to Jason, but she said she didn't want them to know so it was the only other thing we could think of to do.'

'But at what cost to yourself?'

'It was nothing,' he said softly. 'I wasn't hurt. I could only have been hurt if I'd loved her. I didn't love Judith that way. Oh, she was sweet and good and kind. But she was never my wife. She loved Steven's father to the end of her life. I knew that. She never told me who he was. I thought it was Philip but I respected her privacy and never asked. She never told Philip about his son. I don't know why she thought he wouldn't marry her—I found out last night that he was killed in a road accident on his way to see Steven. The only person who knew was Judith's father. She told him all about it in a letter a month before she died. He didn't tell Philip until the morning you and he were to be married. He didn't want Philip ruining your life as well.'

She put a stricken hand to her face and her breath rattled harshly in her throat. 'Why didn't Philip tell me?' she whispered brokenly. 'Why did he leave me at the church waiting for him, wondering what went wrong? Why didn't he have the decency to tell me?'

David watched her, the lines of his face carved with compassion. 'Who can say why he chose to do it that way? He did tell your father, though, and look what it did to him. Maybe he was afraid it would kill you.'

Her head jerked back and all her breath left her and she began to shake. 'All this time Daddy knew? Oh David! He never told me!'

He took an involuntary step towards her, opening his arms wide. She kept looking at him, not daring to move or speak or breathe. Then somehow she was in his arms and he was crushing her to him. His hands were warmly running up and down her spine, stilling her shudders. Burying his face in the side of her neck, his voice was low, almost contemplative. 'In one way or another, Philip's life is entwined with ours: you loved him, he loved Judith, I love their son. I couldn't help but see the way you watched Steven. I was always afraid one day you'd see Philip in him and then I'd lose you.'

'Oh, David.' She clung to him, pressing herself to his length. 'Philip was never the problem. He wouldn't have come between us. I thought I had no right to love you because of Sharon. The smiles you shared—the soulful looks she gave you—you took her places——' she made them sound like accusations.

He leaned back a little and looked at her flaming face. 'I always asked you but you wouldn't come with us.' Then he chuckled softly. 'Were you jealous, my love?'

Hot tears sprang to her eyes and she buried her face in his chest. 'Insanely,' she whispered.

'Good.' His grin was self-satisfied as he tightened his arms around her, shaping her softness to the hard length of him. 'But you don't ever have to be jealous again. I want to marry you, Caroline. Not because I'm being forced into it but because I choose to make the most beautiful woman in the world mine. Will you marry me and make my life complete?'

'Oh, David!' she whispered fiercely, quivering, clinging to him. 'I already made one mistake. I thought I loved Philip but I was wrong. What if I find I don't really love you either?'

He squeezed her so tightly he nearly cut off her breathing. 'There are no guarantees but I'm willing to take a chance that what we have is something rare and very special. I've opened my heart to you. Won't you open yours to me? I promise I'll never hurt you. If you trust me, together we can find out what love is all about.'

She leaned back and looked at this tall

blond giant of a man, feeling an indescribable something running between them, binding them together. It could have been desire but it was so much more than that. She knew she could trust him completely. That was the part she never wanted to admit before. Philip had destroyed her trust in men. She looked at David now and knew if he asked her, she would go to the ends of the earth for him, do anything he wanted, be everything he desired because he was who he was: a most tender, gentle, loving man.

'Yes, David.' She gave him a rosy, full-blown smile. 'Oh, yes! I want to marry you, to be your wife and Steven's mother.'

His expression had been apprehensive but it slowly cleared and he expelled a short breath and kept looking at her as if he couldn't believe she actually said yes. 'Oh, Caro. *My Caro!*'

The passion flaring between them was a palpable thing and with a stifled groan his mouth helplessly covered her lips, kissing her deeply, hungrily, restlessly, over and over again. His roaming hands moved on the softness of her body, following the curve of her back and spine and hips, making her tingle with pleasure in a hundred different places. 'I've wanted you forever,' he murmured into her mouth, 'and now you're mine!'

She arched herself into the hard strength

of him, holding nothing back, wanting to give him everything with all her generous nature. Nothing else existed but this moment. The past was gone. All the lonely emptiness they both had known was replaced by a togetherness that would last a lifetime.

Later that morning they floated hand in hand to the village church where their family had gathered earlier on Grandy's assurance that his granddaughter wasn't a total ninny.

With a smug twisted smile, he watched Caroline and David walk down the middle aisle together and make their vows to love, honour and cherish each other for the rest of their lives.

Get this book FREE!

Mail to:
Harlequin Reader Service

In the U.S.	In Canada
2504 West Southern Ave.	P.O. Box 2800, Postal Station A
Tempe, AZ 85282	5170 Yonge St., Willowdale, Ont. M2N 6J3

YES! I want to be one of the first to discover **Harlequin American Romance.** Send me FREE and without obligation *Twice in a Lifetime.* If you do not hear from me after I have examined my FREE book, please send me the 4 new **Harlequin American Romances** each month as soon as they come off the presses. I understand that I will be billed only $2.25 for each book (total $9.00). There are no shipping or handling charges. There is no minimum number of books that I have to purchase. In fact, I may cancel this arrangement at any time. *Twice in a Lifetime* is mine to keep as a FREE gift, even if I do not buy any additional books. 154 BPA BPGE

Name (please print)

Address Apt. no.

City State/Prov. Zip/Postal Code

Signature (If under 18, parent or guardian must sign.)

This offer is limited to one order per household and not valid to current Harlequin American Romance subscribers. We reserve the right to exercise discretion in granting membership. If price changes are necessary, you will be notified.

AMR-SUB-2R